Sneak Attack

"You hidin', Slocum? From what I heard about you, I wouldn't expect you to squat in the dark pissin' yourself in fear."

Even though Slocum knew damn well that Milt was just trying to bait him into coming out so he could get his head blown off, those words still made him want to break from cover just to shut Milt's fat mouth for good.

But Slocum didn't have to.

Suddenly, silently, a figure lunged in the darkness and pounced on Milt. That silent movement, more than the shape, let Slocum know who it was.

"What in the hell?" Milt squawked as he was brought down to the ground. Daniel had dragged him down and straddled his chest to rain a series of furious blows down on him, but Milt still couldn't get a good enough look at his attacker to decide if he was man or beast.

"Get this son of a bitch offa me!" Milt screamed.

Slocum winced as one powerful punch cracked against Milt's jaw and snapped his head to one side. "Sure," Slocum said while watching Daniel beat Milt some more. "Just as soon as I stop pissing myself in fear."

DON'T MISS THESE
ALL-ACTION WESTERN SERIES
FROM THE BERKLEY PUBLISHING GROUP

THE GUNSMITH by J. R. Roberts
Clint Adams was a legend among lawmen, outlaws, and ladies.
They called him . . . the Gunsmith.

LONGARM by Tabor Evans
The popular long-running series about Deputy U.S. Marshal
Custis Long—his life, his loves, his fight for justice.

SLOCUM by Jake Logan
Today's longest-running action Western. John Slocum rides a
deadly trail of hot blood and cold steel.

BUSHWHACKERS by B. J. Lanagan
An action-packed series by the creators of Longarm! The rous-
ing adventures of the most brutal gang of cutthroats ever
assembled—Quantrill's Raiders.

DIAMONDBACK by Guy Brewer
Dex Yancey is Diamondback, a Southern gentleman turned
con man when his brother cheats him out of the family fortune.
Ladies love him. Gamblers hate him. But nobody pulls one
over on Dex . . .

WILDGUN by Jack Hanson
The blazing adventures of mountain man Will Barlow—from
the creators of Longarm!

TEXAS TRACKER by Tom Calhoun
J.T. Law: the most relentless—and dangerous—manhunter in
all Texas. Where sheriffs and posses fail, he's the best man to
bring in the most vicious outlaws—for a price.

JAKE LOGAN

SLOCUM
AND THE MISTY
CREEK MASSACRE

J
JOVE BOOKS, NEW YORK

THE BERKLEY PUBLISHING GROUP
Published by the Penguin Group
Penguin Group (USA) Inc.
375 Hudson Street, New York, New York 10014, USA
Penguin Group (Canada), 90 Eglinton Avenue East, Suite 700, Toronto, Ontario M4P 2Y3, Canada
(a division of Pearson Penguin Canada Inc.)
Penguin Books Ltd., 80 Strand, London WC2R 0RL, England
Penguin Group Ireland, 25 St. Stephen's Green, Dublin 2, Ireland (a division of Penguin Books Ltd.)
Penguin Group (Australia), 250 Camberwell Road, Camberwell, Victoria 3124, Australia
(a division of Pearson Australia Group Pty. Ltd.)
Penguin Books India Pvt. Ltd., 11 Community Centre, Panchsheel Park, New Delhi—110 017, India
Penguin Group (NZ), 67 Apollo Drive, Rosedale, Auckland 0632, New Zealand
(a division of Pearson New Zealand Ltd.)
Penguin Books (South Africa) (Pty.) Ltd., 24 Sturdee Avenue, Rosebank, Johannesburg 2196,
South Africa

Penguin Books Ltd., Registered Offices: 80 Strand, London WC2R 0RL, England

This is a work of fiction. Names, characters, places, and incidents either are the product of the author's
imagination or are used fictitiously, and any resemblance to actual persons, living or dead, business
establishments, events, or locales is entirely coincidental.

SLOCUM AND THE MISTY CREEK MASSACRE

A Jove Book / published by arrangement with the author

PRINTING HISTORY
Jove edition / March 2012

Copyright © 2012 by Penguin Group (USA) Inc.
Cover illustration by Sergio Giovine.

ISBN: 978-0-515-15048-3

JOVE®
Jove Books are published by The Berkley Publishing Group,
a division of Penguin Group (USA) Inc.,
375 Hudson Street, New York, New York 10014.
JOVE® is a registered trademark of Penguin Group (USA) Inc.
The "J" design is a trademark of Penguin Group (USA) Inc.

PRINTED IN THE UNITED STATES OF AMERICA

10 9 8 7 6 5 4 3 2 1

1

DODGE CITY, KANSAS

Slocum awoke to a bucketful of water being tossed onto his face from on high. His feet thrashed against gritty soil, and his head knocked against a patch of ground that was softened somewhat by the jacket he'd rolled up and placed there the night before. "Son of a bitch!" he snarled while reaching for the holster strapped around his waist. Fortunately for the person holding the empty bucket, that holster was as empty as Slocum's pockets.

The woman holding the bucket glared down at him through eyes that were narrowed by the bright prairie sun. "Watch your mouth," she warned, "or I'll go back to the pump, fill this bucket, and douse you again!"

"What's wrong with you?" Slocum asked while still feeling for his gun. "Can't a man get a moment's rest without being accosted?"

"A moment's rest is one thing. A few hours of rest is reasonable considering the night you must have had, but it's been a lot longer than that, which means it's time for you to move along."

It took a few moments for Slocum to sit up straight and rub his head. His hat was missing, along with his watch and one boot. "I ain't bothering anyone," he said in a string of words that dripped from his mouth like tree sap.

"So you say. I can smell you from inside and it isn't pleasant."

Slocum lifted an arm and sniffed under it. The breath he pulled in through his nostrils caused his chest to swell painfully before catching in the back of his throat. "How about you go back to that pump and reload? Maybe another shower is all I need."

"That won't do a damn thing about your breath," she said while cocking her hip and holding the bucket by its rope handle. "Just being this close to you makes it feel like I was the one to pour half a bottle of whiskey down my throat."

Chuckling at the modest estimate of how much he'd had to drink, Slocum dragged himself to his feet and dusted himself off. Every swat against his jeans or sides only served to expand the dirty cloud surrounding him. "What time is it?"

"Right about noon."

"What day?"

She shook her head as if she was looking at a dog that had gotten its head stuck in the opening of a chicken coop. "Monday."

"Least it ain't Sunday," Slocum offered with a crooked grin.

"Sure. Sleeping through the Lord's day in a drunken heap is real good for the soul. Just collect your things and get off of my property."

Slocum looked in the direction that she'd nodded to find his missing boot sitting on top of his hat. Either that had been his first attempt at a pillow or it had been his way of using one to keep the other from blowing away. After sweeping up his hat and slapping it onto his head, he hopped on one foot so he could get into his boot. "I'm not some sort of transient."

"Could've fooled me."

"Honestly. I just fell onto a patch of bad luck."

After starting to walk toward the large building that faced Chestnut Street, the woman turned on the balls of her feet and asked, "You know who are the first men to say that sort of thing? Transients."

"Guess you have me there. I hope I didn't inconvenience you."

"Soon as you move along and stop stinking up the front of my business, you won't be bothering me anymore."

"Yeah," Slocum sighed as he looked up to study a sign nailed to the front of that building that read, Lucky Days Stable. It was a large, well-maintained structure that gave off a very familiar mix of scents. "About your business. I was wondering if I might impose on you a bit more."

She angled her head slightly and put on an expression that made it seem as if she'd caught another unwelcome sample of his stench. Standing with a confidence that came from within, she planted her feet as if she owned the Lucky Days Stable, the street, and the bedrock below it. "Something tells me I don't want to hear what's coming next."

Doing his best to look either handsome or friendly, Slocum said, "I need a horse."

"You got any money?"

"Let me check." He patted the front of his jeans, stuck his hands into his pockets, and even searched the jacket he'd discovered beneath his head. In an attempt to put a smile onto the woman's face, he turned his jacket upside down and shook it vigorously. When nothing fell out, he said, "Doesn't look like it."

Despite the creases formed in the dirt covering Slocum's face as he grinned at her, the woman wasn't amused. In fact, she couldn't turn away from him quickly enough as she stomped back toward the front door of the stable. "No money. No horse. I run a business, not a charity."

"There's gotta be something you need done around here! I lost a ton of money along with my horse."

"I don't hire transients and I don't hire gamblers." Having reached the door, she stepped inside, set down the bucket she'd been carrying, and faced him. "A town like Dodge City has more than its fill of both and they usually fall on hard times. Some may be good men but none are reliable workers. Learned that lesson well enough the second time one tried to clean me out to pay off some kind of debt."

"You were robbed?"

Stretching an arm so it was out of Slocum's sight for a second, she pulled a shotgun into view from where it had been propped against the door and said, "One robbed me. The one after him only tried."

Slocum held up his hands. No longer trying to charm her, he merely said, "I'm no transient and I'm no gambler."

"How did you wind up sleeping in the dirt outside of my stable?"

"It seemed comfortable when I was full of whiskey."

"And I suppose you lost your watch and gun the same time you took that knock to your head?"

Reaching instinctively to one of many aching spots on his skull, Slocum found a large patch of crusted blood in his hair. That dry crust against his fingers, along with the throbbing pain beneath it, brought back more memories of what had led him to that spot. And the more he recalled, the less he liked what sprang to mind. "All right, so maybe I'm just not a professional gambler. Surely you can't hold one bad night against a man."

She stared at him as if she meant to point the shotgun at his chest, but that intensity quickly faded. The weapon was set back into its spot so she could study him once more while drawing a long breath. "What kind of work can you do?"

"Whatever needs doing."

"What sort of pay are you expecting?" she asked.

"Whatever you think is fair."

At first, the disgruntled expression that drifted onto her face made Slocum think he'd somehow talked himself out of a job. Then, she sighed as if she was more upset with herself when she told him, "I've got some stalls that need cleaning—"

"Done!"

"And," she added while raising a finger to prevent him from cutting her off again, "a loft that needs repairing. One of the support posts was kicked out by a crazy old mule that didn't want to be shoed. Do you know anything about carpentry?"

"I did work of all sorts on my family farm in the Allegheny Mountains." Slocum's casual expression darkened a bit as memories rushed in from all directions. "Had to build and rebuild pretty much everything at one time or another, so yeah. I think I can handle patching up your loft."

Seeing the severity of Slocum's expression caused the woman's to soften. She wasn't about to break out a wide smile, but nodded and extended her hand. "I'm Anne Wolkowski."

"John Slocum," he replied while shaking the hand she offered. Her grip was strong, but not as though she was trying to impress him with it.

"I don't have any money to give you in advance, but I should be able to pay you in a few days. May not be enough to buy a horse for a while, so if that doesn't suit you . . ."

"That suits me just fine," Slocum said. "I could also use a place to sleep." Just as a sour look began to cross Anne's face, he added, "One of the stalls would be fine. Wouldn't be the first time I've slept on a pile of straw."

She looked him over as if waiting for something that would change her mind. Now that Slocum stood there without plastering a grin onto his face, she nodded and stepped aside to clear a path through the doorway. "I've got a few empty stalls right now, but they're dirty. It's your job to rectify that."

"Naturally."

"And if a paying customer wants that stall, you'll have to move your things and find another one."

The smirk that came to Slocum's face now was smaller but genuine when compared to the ones he'd worn earlier. "Seeing as how I barely have any things, that shouldn't be a problem."

When she bowed her head, long strands of straight brown hair fell to cover a portion of her face. Slocum had no doubt the move was intended to obscure the visible signs of a giggle that rustled in the back of her throat. "I pay my hands by results, not by time put in. Start when you like, and when I have enough to divvy out, I'll reimburse you for what you got done."

Slocum placed a hand upon the exterior of the building beside the door frame. Rather than take a single step inside, he used his other hand to tip his battered hat. "Much obliged. I'll get started as soon as I check in on some other unfinished business."

"Business that's more important than doing the job you just about begged me to give you?"

"Afraid so, but don't worry. I doubt it'll take more than a minute or two."

The friendliness that had been on her face a few moments ago evaporated quicker than alcohol spilled onto a stovepipe. Without a word, she moved away from the door and slammed it shut. Slocum couldn't make out the words she muttered, but was fairly certain they weren't complimentary. He put the stable behind him and headed toward Third Avenue.

Dodge City was seldom quiet, but this time of day was filled with noises that appealed more to common folk than the bawdy commotion erupting from the saloon district at night. Horses pulled carts and wagons from one storefront to another while some carried lone riders into or out of the town limits. Most people's eyes darted in every direction, looking for familiar faces or signs of trouble. Considering how many souls resided in Dodge, something was bound to happen at any given time. For some, that was a trial. For others, it was a reason to come to town in the first place. John Slocum could sympathize with either end of that argument.

By the time he'd reached Bridge Street, he'd given his pockets and person a more thorough once-over. Unfortunately, there wasn't much of a difference since the last time he'd examined them. Empty was empty no matter which way you cut it. Now that the blood was flowing a bit quicker through his veins and a good amount of fresh air had brushed over his face, Slocum's senses were fully returning to him to fill in some gaps as to what had landed him on the street in front of the Lucky Days Stable. They also reminded him that the air in Dodge City wasn't exactly fresh under the best of circumstances.

Sounds of men's voices and a piano player from a nearby saloon jarred memories of when he'd recently been in the Dodge House Hotel and Saloon.

The taste of stale whiskey in the back of his mouth harkened back to all the bottles he'd helped drain during his most recent stay there.

The feel of the rough, uneven ground beneath his feet as he cut through Tin Pot Alley reminded him of a few nights back when he'd staggered drunkenly in search of a place to lay his aching head.

But it was the three men standing in the lot near the end of Military Avenue that filled in the rest of the gaps. All of those memories coalesced around the sight of the horse tied to the post directly behind those men. It was the same horse that he'd ridden across the plains of Kansas.

"Well, well," one of the men said. "What have we here? Come back for another game?" He was a tall fellow wearing clothes that were freshly pressed, but didn't seem at all fitting upon his bulky frame. A small bowler hat partially covered a lumpy head with hair that sprouted in irregular clumps like grass growing from a poorly tended field. The cocky tone in his voice and wicked glint in his eye marked him as a man who enjoyed watching others suffer. Dodge City was full of ones just like him.

The man beside the well-dressed fellow wore the rumpled garb of a cowboy, complete with a leather vest that was kept open to display a double rig holster strapped around his waist. Mismatched pistols hung at his sides, both of which looked to have gotten plenty of use. Without any hair or whiskers to cover his face or scalp, a myriad of scars were on prominent display. Some raked across a cheek while others were left behind in spots where chunks of his chin or jaw had been cut or carved away by blade or bullet. He scowled at Slocum as if every last one of those scars still gave him a lingering pain.

"Hello, John," the third man said. "I thought you'd left town." Unlike the other two, he didn't move an inch in response to Slocum's arrival. His suit was obviously more expensive than the first fellow's and was tailored to hang perfectly over a pudgy body. Slocum didn't need to see the bulge from a holster or scabbard to know the man was armed.

"How am I supposed to leave, Cameron?" Slocum asked. "You stole my horse."

Reaching back to pat the animal directly behind him, the pudgy man said, "Won it. Just because you were drunk doesn't mean your bets weren't valid."

"And what about the money that was in my pockets?"

"You lost that, too. Or don't you recall?"

At that moment, Slocum did recall digging into his pockets sometime during that game to remove some of his cash to cover a bet on a ten-high straight, which had been cracked by a luckier player. Slocum chalked that one up to the whiskey, but knew he could never get drunk enough to lose the money he'd stashed in his boot for expenses. "What about my pistol?" he asked. "You want to try and convince me I lost that on a bet as well?"

Although the big man in the stolen suit began to say something, he was stopped when Cameron placed a hand upon his shoulder. "I didn't see that happen during our game," Cameron said. "But it was never my job to be your guardian angel."

"Yeah," the bald fellow with the double rig proclaimed. "That's me and Fitz's job."

Fitz nodded and straightened lapels that had more elegance than he could ever hope to possess. "Milt and I made it our business to watch you real good, John. Or perhaps you don't recall that either?"

Milt and Fitz. Those names definitely rang a bell inside Slocum's head. In fact, they made him wonder just how much he'd drunk that night for him to have forgotten them in the first place. There was no forgetting them anymore, however. "I recall you two lurking around the poker tables like a pair of ghouls. You also followed me outside when I left the game."

"Left in anything but a straight line, I should add," Cameron said.

Slocum nodded curtly. "Granted. But there's no way in hell I would have left that game without my gun. Even a greener would know better than to walk around Dodge City without protection from assholes like these."

Those words caused Fitz and Milt to strut forward as if they meant to trample Slocum into the dirt.

"Better watch your tone, mister," Milt said as he stepped up to knock his chest against Slocum's. "A greener don't know nothin' about anything, so they get some slack. Since that ain't what you are, you don't get an inch."

"Don't need any," Slocum replied as he snapped his hand out to pluck the gun from one of Milt's holsters. The pistol was on Milt's left, which meant it was the smaller of the two. Even so, the .38 fit nicely in Slocum's hand as he flipped it to slide three fingers around its grip and another upon its trigger. "That green enough for you?"

Although Milt's eyes burned with an angry fire, his body knew better than to make another move. One hand hovered over the .44 holstered on his right hip while the other remained pressed tightly against the spot where the .38 had been.

Suddenly, Fitz decided to speak like a man who belonged in the suit that hung on him. "No need for all of this, John. That was a hard night for a lot of folks."

"Shut the hell up," Slocum snapped. "I'm also missing my watch, some money, and my gun. I may not recall everything that happened when I stepped out of the Dodge House, but I know I had my watch and gun. Perhaps I should ask around inside the Dodge House to see if anyone else remembers much from that night."

Cameron stepped to one side and swept an arm toward the back end of the hotel as if he'd been large enough to keep Slocum from getting to it before. "Go right ahead. Just about everyone in there knows me, so you shouldn't have to search long for your answers."

Still keeping the .38 pointed at Milt, Slocum said, "I'm recalling more and more the longer I stand here. For one thing, I distinctly remember walking down Tin Pot Alley and not making it out before I found myself on the ground."

"You drank like there was a hole in your throat," Fitz chuckled. "Any man tends to fall down a lot under them circumstances."

Slocum reached back with his free hand to touch the crusty spot on the back of his head. One careful fingertip upon that spot sent a stabbing jolt of pain through his skull that caused one eye to twitch. "Unless the whiskey busted me in the head, I'd say there's another reason I took that tumble."

Growing comfortable behind his two enforcers, Cameron

drew a cigar from a breast pocket and placed it between his teeth. "If you believe you were robbed, perhaps you should contact the authorities?"

"No need for that. I'll find out what happened soon enough and deal with the son of a bitch myself."

Fitz stepped up so he was shoulder to shoulder with Milt to form a veritable wall of meat in cheap clothing. "You sure you want to go down that road? Seems like an awful lot of trouble to go through for a missing watch, a few dollars, and a pistol."

"I don't give a damn if it was just the lint at the bottom of my pockets that was taken. I don't like anyone thinking they can walk all over me and get away with it."

"I don't like someone stealing from me neither," Milt said. "Hand back my pistol."

Slocum didn't so much as glance down at the beefy hand Milt extended toward him palm-up. "If I find out you had nothing to do with robbing me after I walked down Tin Pot Alley, I'll deliver it to you myself. And if I find out something different," he said with a wolfish grin, "I'll jam it down your throat."

2

When he stepped into the Dodge House, Slocum felt every second of the hours that had passed since his last visit. The ache in his head and stomach made it feel as if his night of drunken debauchery had worked him over with a shovel. Upon reaching the bar in the saloon, he grunted, "Coffee. Black."

The man who stepped up to fill the order had thinning brown hair and weighed no more than ninety pounds soaking wet.

"You're not the usual barkeep," Slocum pointed out.

"There's a few of us that work here," the little man said. "Which one are you thinking of?"

"Can't recall his name, but he was working Friday and Saturday night."

"That'd be Everett."

"Know how I could catch up with him?"

"Come back on Friday or Saturday. That's the only time he works here." Having poured a cup of steaming brew from the pot behind the bar, the skinny fellow set the cup down without taking his hand from it. "Sorry, mister. Can't open an account for one cup of coffee."

Slocum couldn't decide which made him more cross: the fact that the barkeep assumed he couldn't pay for the coffee or that the assumption was correct. "Do you know where I might find Everett now?"

"Long as he shows up here when he's supposed to, I don't give a damn where he goes."

"All right, then," Slocum said while doing his best not to stare longingly at the hot drink in front of him. "Guess I'll just get my coffee elsewhere."

Obviously accustomed to dealing with men who were down on their luck without making them feel even worse, the bartender set the cup under the bar without any more fuss. "Feel free to stop by again if you like."

Slocum was about to walk out through the door that opened onto Front Street when he diverted his path toward a desk where hotel business was conducted. An attractive woman in her late thirties sat behind it and brightened up the instant Slocum walked toward her. The pleasant expression on her face dimmed once she got a closer look at him. "Mr. Slocum?" she asked. "Where have you been?"

"Long story."

"You don't look so good."

"I feel worse. You wouldn't happen to have the key to my room, would you?"

She smiled and turned toward the pegboard behind her. "After your card game the other night, I heard you left the Dodge House and didn't come back until . . . well . . . now. Did you find some more pleasant company?"

The fact of the matter was that he'd only just remembered that he had a hotel room at all. Between the whiskey and the knock to the head, his thoughts were taking their own sweet time to come into focus. "No, I didn't."

"Perhaps I can do something about that."

Slocum would have needed to be hit on the head many more times for him to forget about Estrella. She was a smoky Mexican beauty with thick black hair and eyes that were as lively as they were promising. She'd been the one to check him into the Dodge House and wish him luck whenever he'd gone downstairs for a game. Since he'd been in Dodge City for only a week or so, the familiarity she used when addressing him spoke of something more than courtesy shown to a paying customer. "Yes," Slocum replied. "Perhaps you can. I could use a bath."

"Should I tack that on to your bill?"

"Only if you can guarantee the water won't be cold."

"I think I can arrange that," she told him in a way that made a good portion of Slocum's pains melt away.

"Do you know anything about the bartenders that work here?"

"Some."

"What about Everett?"

She considered that for a moment before shrugging and saying, "I don't think he's working right now. Did you check the next room?"

Estrella may have been beautiful, but she wasn't the brightest light in the sky. "Yeah. The bar was the first place I looked for the bartender."

"Then you should try Stella's. It's a steak place down on Railroad Street. That's where I have to send for him when he's late for work here."

"That's very helpful. Can I have my key?"

She handed it over with a promising smile. "What about that bath?"

They hadn't talked much, but Slocum had been sure to compliment her dress or engage in some form of flirtatious small talk every time he'd passed that desk. The night when he'd indulged in so much whiskey and cards would have been the one for him to invite her upstairs. Apparently, that wasn't such an uncommon idea. "Since you can guarantee it'll be hot, I suppose I can take one when I come back."

"Good," she said with a distinct grimace, "because you smell like you slept in a trash heap."

So much for the groundwork of charm and flirtatious small talk.

Stella's Chop House was a fairly large place on Railroad Street that looked as if it had been built with some sort of warehouse in mind. The interior consisted of one large dining room with a back wall that was broken up by a small door and a long opening that must have looked into a kitchen. Although the bare wooden tables and irregularly shaped chairs weren't appealing to the eye, the scents filling the place put a hungry smile onto Slocum's face. The moment he took more than two steps inside, he was greeted by a smiling woman with a thick head of silver hair bound into a tight bun.

"Welcome to Stella's," she said. "You here for lunch, early dinner, or late breakfast?"

"I'm here to meet a man I was told might be found here. His name's Everett."

"Sure, he's one of my cooks. Works the early shift, but he should still be cleaning up." Turning toward the back, she shouted, "Everett!"

The man who responded to the summons was a few inches shorter than Slocum and younger by no more than six or seven years, but had the droopy eyes and slow shuffle of a man in his sixties. Slocum recognized him the moment Everett stepped out from the kitchen. He must have recognized Slocum as well because his eyes widened to almost comical proportions and he darted through the door, vaulted a table, and knocked over half a dozen chairs in his haste to get to an exit that was marked by a sign directing customers to the outhouses.

Acting on raw instinct, Slocum tore after the cook. There were a few diners in the establishment, but they either stood up or scooted their chairs away to clear a path through the room. The folks wearing the blandest expressions in the midst of that sudden burst of excitement had more than likely been in Dodge City for the longest amount of time.

Slocum charged through the restaurant fast enough to reach the side door before it had stopped rattling after Everett had burst through it. The cook bolted past the outhouses like his tail feathers were on fire, heading east toward the railroad depot. When he turned to get a quick look behind him, he was nearly trampled by a horse being ridden into town. Although he managed to avoid that undignified end, he was off balance and panicked enough to slam into the post of a general store's awning. Everett bounced off that, cursing to high heaven, and moved on.

Keeping his eyes focused intently on his target, Slocum cut through the pedestrian traffic like a hot knife through butter, weaving between the horses and carriages being driven down Railroad Street. Keeping one hand on the grip of his holstered .38, he used the other to reach for Everett's shoulder as he closed in on the disoriented cook. Everett pulled his wits together quickly enough once he spotted Slocum bearing down on him. Shoving past a few concerned citizens who'd seen his collision with the post, Everett darted away as if he'd been launched from a catapult. Some of the people who'd seen Everett running like a madman after hurting himself stepped in to block Slocum's progress. They tried to stop him or ask what he thought he was doing, but Slocum shoved past them without doing any harm.

If Everett had had any sense, he would have headed toward the larger crowds on Front Street. His only concern was in running fast, which must have been why he chose Military Avenue for his escape route. There were fewer people there, which gave him more room to build up some steam. Of course, that meant Slocum had the same opportunity and he took full advantage of it by churning his legs as fast as they could go. After a dozen or so steps, he fell

into a rhythm that allowed him to once again close the gap
between him and the panicked cook.

Everett knew better than to look over his shoulder again,
but must have heard Slocum's steps drawing closer like a
train rolling over the nearby tracks. His feet pounded against
the ground, kicking up dirt and gravel as his breath churned
within his lungs. Even his arms flailed faster as though making a futile attempt to lift him off the ground and into the
safety of the skies. High hopes weren't going to do much
good now, however. Slocum was within inches of him and
the cook was running out of steam.

Now that he was close enough, Slocum reached out with
both hands and strained even harder to get a grip on Everett's shirt. His first attempts came up short and the next few
swipes made him wonder if the other man had eyes in the
back of his head to let him know exactly when to squirm
forward or dash a little faster. Slocum's knees blazed with
fiery pain as he pushed his aching body even harder. His
arms strained with the effort of extending toward something
that remained just out of their reach. When he made his next
attempt to grab Everett, his fingers brushed against the
cook's back. That only served to ignite something else inside
the fleeing man and he lurched forward into a series of steps
that verged on spastic.

Slocum pushed a bit harder as well while taking a quick
survey of the road directly in front of Everett. There was a
rough patch coming up, so he decided to try and add a little
strategy into the mix.

"Hey!" Slocum shouted. "I think this belongs to you!"

There was nothing in Slocum's hands or anything in his
possession that he thought could have belonged to Everett,
but the claim sparked the other man's interest just enough
for him to glance back and take his eyes away from the path
before him. By the time he turned around again, his feet
were crossing the rough patch Slocum had picked out.

Everett's feet skidded. He stumbled forward, reached out

with both hands to brace himself for a potential fall, and then regained his footing. The diversion hadn't tripped him up, but his speed had dipped just enough for Slocum to make one last push. Channeling everything he could into his legs, Slocum lunged at Everett's back with both arms outstretched. "Gotcha!" he said the moment his fingers closed around a sizable chunk of the other man's shirt.

No matter how badly Everett wanted to keep moving, Slocum's grip was too strong for him to do so. His arms and legs continued to flail, but he wasn't going anywhere. A few seconds later, Everett was swung to one side and tossed to the ground like a sack of potatoes.

"Why the . . . hell were you . . ." was all Slocum could say before Everett rolled over with enough force to twist his shirt free. The sudden jerking motion pulled Slocum in close enough to catch the wild fist that was thrown at his face. The other man's knuckles glanced off Slocum's jaw, snapping his head to one side.

The swing may have connected, but it threw Everett once more off his balance, and he was all too willing to flop onto his belly and crawl away. As soon as Slocum started to chase after him again, he was discouraged by a few donkey kicks Everett threw directly behind him.

His jaw still stinging from the punch, Slocum scurried around Everett and swatted aside one kick before it caught him below the belt. This time when he grabbed hold of Everett, he slammed him with enough force to drive the crawling man's face into the gravel. As satisfying as it would have been to make him taste some more little rocks, Slocum pulled Everett up.

"And don't take another—"

Once again, Everett cut Slocum off with a wild punch. His fist didn't make contact with anything but air, but his elbow cracked against Slocum's ribs to send a sharp spiking pain through his side. Since he already had a hold of him,

Slocum allowed Everett to twist around so he was in prime position for the knee that was driven into his stomach. When Slocum delivered the short, pounding blow, Everett crumpled.

"All right," Slocum said while straightening the other man up as if he was a large doll. "Why the hell did you run?"

"Why the hell did you chase me?"

"I just came to that steak house to talk and you bolted."

"You could've just let me go!" Everett whined.

"Well, I may not wear a tin star pinned to my chest, but I've learned a thing or two from lawmen. One of the first is that innocent men usually don't have a reason to run from people paying them a visit."

"I know why you were coming after me!"

"Really? Why?"

Everett didn't seem anxious to answer that question. Since he wasn't alert and barely able to stand upon his trembling legs, the cook fell onto his backside when he was shoved again. Looming over him, Slocum said, "I just wanted to ask you about something that happened the night you were working at the Dodge House. There was a card game. Afterward, I . . ."

Slocum wasn't cut short this time. Instead, he stopped talking because Everett had turned and tried to crawl away. Tired of the constant interruptions, Slocum picked him up by what would have been the scruff of Everett's neck, pulled him to his feet, and shoved him against the closest wall. The entire wooden structure rattled when Everett hit it and the stench coming from within made it more than obvious that it was an outhouse.

"You know what happened, don't you?" Slocum growled.

Everett tried to turn away, but there was nowhere for him to go. When he twisted his head to look in another direction, he was jarred by the impact of his back pounding against the wooden wall.

"Don't you?" Slocum demanded.

"Yes! I'm sorry! It was just the usual arrangement!"

"You had an arrangement with Cameron?"

"No," Everett replied. "With Milt."

Even though he knew the name, Slocum couldn't believe that the older gunman was the one he was after. "You mean the man who wears two guns and has a face full of scars?"

"That's him all right. He pays me to steer men his way so they can be jumped in Tin Pot Alley."

Slocum squinted as he went through the painful process of sifting through memories that rattled inside his throbbing head. He'd already pieced together portions of the card game and a few moments from his drunken walk from the Dodge House. Staring at Everett allowed him to focus on the few times he'd engaged the bartender in conversation. It was still hazy.

"You told me to go down Tin Pot Alley?" Slocum guessed.

"No, I told you that Estrella rented a room down there and wanted to meet you."

While Slocum's guess hadn't seemed like something that would have gotten him into that alley, what Everett said made a lot more sense.

"You were buying another bottle of whiskey and asked where she was," the cook continued.

It was all rushing back to him now. Slocum closed his eyes and said, "Second building on the left at the top of a set of narrow stairs."

"That's right. That's what I told you."

"And the deal with Milt?"

"It's a standing offer," Everett said. "I steer anyone having a good night down that alley so Milt and Fitz can bushwhack them."

"I may have been drunk as a skunk, but I know I wasn't having a good night at that game."

"Maybe not, but he knew who you are. He heard about some of the men you killed in New Mexico and those gunmen you hunted down in the Badlands."

Slocum had a vague idea of what Everett was talking about, but his hesitance wasn't due to any knock to the head. There had just been too many hunts in his lifetime to sort them all out by location. The ghosts of the dead would always hang over his head regardless of where they were buried.

"Were those dead men friends of his?" Slocum asked.

"I don't know. I don't think so. He didn't seem angry about them's that was killed. Talked like he admired you. Asked me if I was certain you were the real John Slocum and not just some asshole trying to pass himself off under that name. All I said was that you were answering to that name all night long, so he told me to try and steer you down Tin Pot Alley."

When Slocum had realized he'd been robbed, he was angry at himself just as much as he was angry at the robbers. Upon reacquainting himself with Cameron and the two gunmen working as hired muscle for the gambler, Slocum wanted nothing more than to make sure they were behind the robbery so he could fully savor taking back what they'd stolen either from their pockets or out of their hides. This new bit of information cast a different light on the matter, however.

"What else did you tell Milt?" Slocum asked.

"He didn't ask much of anything else."

"Does he know I was staying at the Dodge House?"

Everett shrugged as if he was getting comfortable dangling from Slocum's fists. "Probably. Was it supposed to be a secret?"

"Where can I find him?"

"Cameron's either at the Dodge House or the Long Branch, where all the big games are played."

"No," Slocum said, emphasizing the word by giving him

a single, jarring shake. "I mean where can I find Milt or Fitz when they're not out hunting for easy prey? Tell me where they live, where they eat, which barber they go to, just tell me where I can find them outside of a saloon."

"I don't know! I swear to Christ! They're always with Cameron."

All Slocum needed to do was place one hand upon the grip of the holstered .38 for Everett to start shaking like a leaf.

"I told you already!" the cook squealed. "I don't know!"

Now that the pounding thump of his heartbeat had eased up, Slocum could hear hushed voices encroaching on him from several different angles. Other folks were taking an interest in his conversation, and he even heard a few whispered mentions of fetching the law to come and deal with the situation.

Before he ran out of time to question Everett, Slocum asked, "Who the hell is Milt anyway?"

"Milt Connoway. He's lived in Dodge on and off for the last couple of years. Came back around not too long ago, working the saloons on his own before throwing in with Mr. Cameron. I do most of my work at the chop house. All I see of Milt or Cameron or that other one is when they ask me to do that little bit of work for them."

"Little bit of work, huh?" Slocum said as his grip tightened around the front of Everett's shirt. "I got knocked on the head so hard that I damn near forgot about the last two days of my life!"

"Folks get bushwhacked all the time around here! Hell, sometimes it's the law that does it. People are robbed no matter what."

"So you might as well make a few dollars off of it, huh?"

"Well . . ."

"Never mind," Slocum snapped. "Don't answer that question or I won't be able to keep from beating you to a pulp in front of all these people."

Everett started to look around at the gathering crowd, but was brought back to the matter at hand when Slocum pulled him in close enough to be heard when he dropped his voice to a low rumble. "Your little side business of steering folks to get robbed ends right now, you understand?"

Everett nodded.

"And if Milt or anyone else connected to those two comes up to you asking for leads, I want to know about it. You tell them whatever you have to in order to buy some time without setting anyone else up for a fall. Don't let them know you're out of the arrangement. Just get word back to me and I'll let you know what to do from there. Got it?"

Everett nodded again.

"You'd best do exactly what I told you," Slocum warned. "Those back-shooting bastards chose the wrong man to rob. They'll learn that lesson soon enough. If I have to straighten you out again, you'll be hard pressed to find three bones in your body that ain't snapped in two."

"So you ain't gonna kill me now or . . . break anything?"

"I'm letting you off this time," Slocum said with a hint of warning in his voice. "Will those assholes be at the Dodge House tonight?"

"Yeah, but I won't."

"Yes you will. You'll find a way to get behind that bar. I don't care how you do it or who you've got to beg, but you'll be there to tell them exactly what I want you to tell them." Leaning in even closer, Slocum added, "And let me make one thing perfectly clear. I don't give a damn if you see a man stagger into that saloon with gold nuggets spilling from his pockets. You won't set up one more soul to get jumped in Tin Pot Alley. Got that?"

"Y-Y-Yes."

"All right, then." Like any good fisherman, Slocum let his minnow go only after he was sure the hook was set good and tight.

And like any good piece of live bait, Everett couldn't wriggle away fast enough.

As the petrified cook darted toward Front Street, Slocum tipped his hat to the small crowd that had gathered nearby and strolled toward Military Avenue.

3

It was a fairly good walk to Chestnut Street, which did wonders to clear Slocum's head. The day was taking on a dry heat that was driven off nicely by the many awnings lining the boardwalk. Unlike the wetlands of Louisiana or the mountainous regions of the Appalachians, the heat wasn't a wet, clinging substance that followed a man no matter where he sought refuge. The Kansas sun shone down with a powerful intensity to bake the dirt without having the teeth of an oppressive humidity. By the time Slocum returned to the Lucky Days Stable, he'd managed to piece together even more of what had happened on the night when he'd taken his unfortunate stroll down Tin Pot Alley. It was an ugly picture that left him feeling angrier at himself for allowing it to develop in the first place.

Anne was brushing down a fine-looking dun inside the stable when Slocum knocked on the frame of the open door. She didn't bother looking over at him before saying, "You seem even worse than you did this morning."

"Can you smell me from there?"

"Yes," she chuckled, "but that's not what I meant. I saw

you walking down the street. Looks like there was a lot on your mind."

"A lot's coming back to me."

"Like why you curled up in a ditch when you had a perfectly good room at the Dodge House?"

Despite everything else that was troubling him, Slocum couldn't help laughing at that. "Did you know about that the whole time?"

"You were flopped over in front of my stable for a whole day. Covered in filth and not moving. I thought you were dead. I tried splashing some water on you several times on Sunday, but that just got you riled up for a minute or two." As she spoke, her hands went through the motions of brushing the dun. Both she and the horse were soothed by the simple chore. "I went to the marshal to have you removed and he recognized your face. Asked me if I could let you sleep where you lay until you woke up in the mud with a headache that made you want to blow your own head off your shoulders. His words, by the way."

Slocum shook his head and sighed. "Of course."

"Seeing as how I don't run a hotel and the sight of you drove away at least one paying customer, I splashed you again sometime after that. If you would have woken up in a more agreeable state, I would have explained things to you. As it was, I didn't appreciate being threatened on my own property."

"I explained myself," he told her. "And I apologized. Didn't I?"

"I can't recall."

"Just like I couldn't recall my room at the Dodge House right away. And I'm apologizing now." Removing his hat and sweeping it across the front of his body in a formal bow, he said, "I apologize, ma'am, for all the grief I may have caused you."

Anne put her back to him as she continued to brush the

horse. Despite all of that posturing, she couldn't keep him from seeing the grin that drifted across her face. "I take it you won't be needing to sleep in one of my stalls."

"No, but I will be needing a horse."

"I thought you would have had one put up near the Dodge House."

"Lost it in that poker game."

She swiveled around on the balls of her feet, looking angrier now than at any other point since he'd met her. "Your horse was stolen along with your gun?"

"No, I lost the horse fair and square. I remember as much now, which is part of the reason why my head keeps hurting so badly. A bad night in poker can be worse than several knocks to the head."

"Well, I have a cure for that. If you still need to earn some money, you can start right now." She took hold of one of his hands and slapped the brush into it. "Finish up with this lady and clean up those other two. Then you can scoop out the stalls."

"Right now?"

"Did you have any better plans?"

It was still early afternoon, and Slocum knew it would be a while before his bait would collect himself enough to show his face at the Dodge House. "Actually," he said, "I was hoping to get some rest. My head's still splitting."

"You've had too much rest," she replied. "That's why you feel so tired. As for the headache, I'll whip something up for that. Just get to brushing."

Since Slocum didn't have a chance to protest before she marched out of the stable, he peeled off his jacket, hung it over the gate to a nearby stall, rolled up his sleeves, and got to brushing. The simple task did wonders for his aching back and limbs. After no more than a few minutes, the throbbing behind his temples died down and muscles that had been tender after an uncomfortable night's sleep were warmed up again. Compared to the exercise he'd gotten chasing after Everett, this was like a firm massage that soaked all the way down to his joints.

Once the dun was brushed, Slocum moved toward a spotted mare two stalls down. She stamped her hooves impatiently and stretched her chin out past the stall to nudge the hand that carried the brush. "Hold on, girl," Slocum said while patting her muzzle. "You're about to get your turn."

Before he'd completed his first stroke with the brush, the side door to the stable was pushed open so Anne could step inside. "She likes you," Anne said. "But don't think you can just ride away with her with nothing but credit."

"I didn't even consider I'd be so lucky."

"Good," she told him while handing over a dented cup that looked more like a large ladle that had gotten its handle ripped off, "because you won't. That string of bad luck may take a turn for the better once you get a sip of this, though."

Slocum took the cup from her and sniffed its contents. At least, he tried to sniff them before the pungent odor of the steam emanating from the murky liquid reached up to slap him in the face harder than a disgruntled debutante. "What in the hell is this concoction?"

"It's a cure for what ails you."

"I've heard that before, but usually from a shady salesman."

"Only I'm telling you the God's honest truth. Stop trying to smell it and drink up."

"But what *is* it?"

"Knowing that won't make it taste any better. Just know that it works." When Slocum stared at her without moving the cup one inch closer to his mouth, she sighed and explained, "Most of the hired hands that have worked for me either came here needing money after spending too much time in the saloon district or wind up going to Front Street the moment I pay them. Either way, they come back to me drunk and try to use that as an excuse to stretch out in a corner somewhere when they should be working."

"So you're telling me I'm not the first man you've awoken using a barrel of water?"

"Not even close to the first, Mr. Slocum."

"Please, call me John."

"All right, John. Drink."

"You swear you're not out to poison me?" he asked.

"Take a look at these stalls. Now take a look at the coats of those horses. There's too much work to be done around here, and I don't have any other hired hands to help me do it. If I meant to poison you, it would be somewhere between the time when the work's done and I get the money to pay you."

"I suppose you make a good point." Slocum lifted the cup in a halfhearted toast, which also served to befoul the air directly in front of his nose. "Care to join me?"

"I'm not the one who needs it."

Without further ado, he brought the cup to his mouth and knocked it back while angling his chin toward the roof. The drink tasted like salty turpentine that had been boiled in a batch of old tomato soup. He had to fight back the urge to spit it out before swallowing his first gulp and was soon glad he did. Although the stuff was atrocious, it somehow pushed down the bile that had been rising up toward the back of his throat ever since he'd opened his eyes that morning. As the fumes permeated his head, they dispersed the pains inside it like smoke that had been chased away by a fan.

Just when he thought he was feeling better, Slocum exhaled and unleashed a horrific torrent of breath. "Good lord," he groaned. "You've got to tell me what's in that!"

"You sure you want to know?"

While Slocum considered that question, he took another sip. This one was just small enough to go down his throat without spending too much time on his tongue and just large enough to do some good once it got down. "Yeah. I wanna know."

"Water, garlic, salt," she said while ticking the ingredients off on her fingers. "Orange rinds, coffee grounds."

"Coffee grounds?" Slocum asked while running his tongue along the grit that coated his back teeth.

"Yes. Also, pepper, celery, ground eggshells—"

"Stop right there," Slocum cut in. "Something tells me you're starting off with the least offensive ingredients and already it sounds like you scraped out your trash and boiled it in tomato juice."

"There *are* tomatoes! Very good."

"Anything else?"

"Yes."

"Fine. It seems to work, so let's just leave it at that. How on earth would you come up with a recipe like that anyway?"

"It started as a way to punish those lazy workers I told you about," she admitted. "The more awful things I poured in, the more good it seemed to do. Finally, I hit upon something that honestly did the trick."

"Must have taken a lot of trial and error."

"There's no shortage of drunkards in Dodge City."

"Well, thanks to your tonic," he said while handing back the cup, "I am no longer one of them. Back to work for me."

"Good. Anything else I can get for you?"

"I learned my lesson with the first thing you got for me, but thanks all the same."

"The marshal had nothing but good things to say about you, John. Anything else I needed to know, you told me just by honoring your promise to come back and do some work for me. At least, that's all I need to know for today."

When he looked at her, Slocum felt even less foggy behind the eyes. They shared a quiet moment before she turned around and left once again through the side door. As if sensing his eyes were still upon her, she stopped and said, "One more thing, John."

"What's that?"

"If you can't afford a bath, I've got a tub you can use."

"Much obliged."

"Don't mistake that for kindness either," she added. "The stink coming off of you is making the horses nervous."

4

Slocum returned to the Dodge House a few hours later. Since he'd already been covered in dirt, blood, and dust, he figured a healthy layer of sweat wouldn't make much difference. When he left the Lucky Days, the horses were brushed and most of the stalls were clean. Now that Anne's putrid tonic had worked its way through his system like acid through a set of rusty pipes, he was starving. There was still work to be done, but she didn't have any problem with letting him get back to it later. And as the sun drew closer to the western horizon, Slocum wanted to be certain everything was in place for dealing with Cameron and his hired guns.

Slocum was out to do more than just reclaim his stolen possessions. Dodge City wasn't just any cow town. It was a point on the map written in bold letters that stood out to everyone from ranchers and land barons to gamblers, killers, and thieves. There were already enough men who knew about Slocum's reputation. Some gave him a wide berth on account of all the men he was rumored to have gunned down, and others sought him out to avenge the real blood debts. Still others hunted him because killing any man with

Slocum's reputation would serve to build up their own name. If he was bushwhacked like a common drunk in Dodge City, word would spread quicker than wildfire and more men would come after him like wolves after catching a whiff of fresh meat. That simply couldn't be allowed. More important, men like Cameron, Milt, or Fitz couldn't be given bragging rights of that magnitude.

The woman behind the front desk in the Dodge House's lobby was a younger girl whom Slocum had seen only once before. Although he couldn't think of her name, she seemed to recognize him well enough. Her eyes snapped open wide and she drew a quick breath to address him the moment he was close enough to hear her voice. "Good day to you, Mr. Slocum," she said.

"Hello. I'm—"

"Here for your bath, no doubt," the girl interrupted. "I was told to get it ready the moment you arrived." She'd already grabbed her master key and was headed for the stairs before she turned back around and asked, "Would you like it now?"

"Yes, I would."

"Good," she said with a smile. "I'll come to collect you when it's ready. Shouldn't be a moment. Will you be waiting in the saloon?"

"No, I don't even want to look at a bottle of whiskey right now. I think I'll step into my room for a spell."

"All right. We have a first-class laundry if you'd like to get your clothes cleaned along with the rest of you."

Already heading for the stairs, Slocum said, "Think I'll just go up to my room, if it's all the same to you."

She pulled in a short breath and did a bad job at hiding the distaste that came along with it. "You really might want to consider using our laundry. I mean, seeing as how you'll be scrubbing up and all."

Slocum brought his sleeve up to his nose and took another whiff. "You're right. I'll send these clothes down as soon as

I'm out of them. If you can't remedy the foul smell, feel free to burn them."

That brought a brighter smile to her face as she rushed away to attend to some other bit of important business.

Slocum's room was number 42, and he went to it without having to think much about where he was going. After climbing up and down the stairs enough times when he'd been drinking or gambling, his feet knew the way. It wasn't often he came to Dodge City, but his visits were always eventful. This time around, he'd treated himself to a room in the town's finest hostelry, which he'd paid for during a run of good luck at the card tables his first night in town. He was already all too familiar with how that luck had turned, and he braced himself for another round of bad news as he reached out to take hold of the handle of the door to Room 42.

Fitting his key into the lock, he imagined varying scenes of upended furniture, clothes scattered about, and whatever remained of his possessions lying on the floor. What he got was a neatly tended room, a bed made up with fresh linens, a basin of clean water on one of the dressers, frilly curtains on the window, and the few possessions he'd brought to town stacked right where he'd left them. His saddlebag was draped over one chair, and a spare set of clothes was folded upon its seat.

Now that he saw the little room, Slocum felt silly for his initial fears. Cameron and his hired guns may have been back-shooting thieves, but there was no reason they'd be interested in stealing another man's clothes. Cameron had won most of the cash from Slocum's pockets as well as the horse he'd ridden in on. Besides that, the Dodge House had a reputation to maintain which wasn't served very well if they made it easy for heavy-handed thieves to get into any of the upstairs rooms.

His foul-smelling clothes came off him like a skin that wasn't quite ready to be shed. His shirt stuck to his back.

His jeans scraped against his legs and he needed to sit upon the edge of his bed in order to pull his boots off his feet. He'd just slipped into a robe that had been hanging on a hook next to the bed when a small set of knuckles rapped against his door. Cinching the robe shut, Slocum crossed the room and opened the door.

The girl from the front desk showed him her usual smile, but her eyes widened and she pulled in a quick breath when she got a look at his bare chest beneath the open folds of the robe. "Your bath is ready," she said.

Since her eyes were still wandering south of his face, he asked, "Care to join me?"

Judging by the rise of her eyebrows and the tone of her laugh, that may not have been such an improbable notion. "I need to get back downstairs, Mr. Slocum. The bathroom is right down this hall on the left. If there's anything else you need, please let me know."

Once she turned around, Slocum was able to watch the sway of her hips and the inviting way her dress rustled against her backside. "I most certainly will," he said to himself.

The carpeting of the hallway felt soft beneath feet that had become accustomed to either slapping against packed earth or being stuffed into a pair of stirrups. The subdued lighting thrown off by lamps fixed to the wall was welcomed by a pair of eyes that had become almost permanently narrowed due to an unforgiving prairie sun. By the time he reached the bathroom, Slocum was in positively good spirits. Those only improved when he opened the door to find his tub situated in a stall that was revealed by a curtain that had been pulled aside. He knew it was his tub for two reasons. First of all, it was the only one filled with steaming hot water. Second, the woman lying naked within that hot water reached out with one hand to beckon for him to approach.

"I've been waiting for you," Estrella said.

Slocum locked the door behind him and then tugged at

the ties of his robe as he crossed the room. "Hope it wasn't for too long. I expect that to still be warm."

"It is," she replied while sitting up so her full, rounded breasts emerged from the water. "I thought you'd be here earlier."

"I've been tending to some business."

"Well, I've got some business I've been meaning to tend to." With that, she climbed out of the tub. Water flowed over skin that was darkened by the sun as well as her Mexican heritage. The fine lines of her body were accented by rivulets that flowed over large, dark nipples to trace lines down her flat stomach all the way to the thatch of hair between her legs. Every step she took made her breasts sway and her hips twitch. By the time she was close enough to touch him, Slocum was fully aroused.

"Is this part of the service offered to all hotel guests?" he asked.

Estrella's fingers wrapped around his erection. The water on her skin allowed her hand to glide easily back and forth as she stroked him. "Only for ones as handsome as you."

"So I'm not the first man you've surprised like this? Perhaps I should be offended by that," Slocum said in a mocking tone.

"Then you can leave." Estrella let him go and turned her back to Slocum as if she had every intention of gathering the dress that was heaped on a nearby stool and returning to her duties.

Slocum allowed his robe to drop to the floor and reached out to place his hands upon her hips. Although Estrella kept moving forward, she didn't try very hard to escape his grasp. When Slocum pulled her close enough for his rigid pole to press against the curve of her buttocks, she responded with a surprised moan and reached back to slide one hand along the side of his face.

"Where do you think you're goin'?" he asked.

"I'm not a whore."

"Never called you one."

"What you said about me treating all of the guests this way is . . ." Her words trailed off when Slocum's hands wandered from her hips to move along her sides and come around to cup her breasts. Closing her eyes, she leaned back against him and slowly ground herself against his stiff member.

Estrella's body was smooth as silk, apart from her nipples, which were erect and hard against his touch. She was tall for a woman and within a few inches of Slocum's height. Therefore, she matched up very well to him, and all she needed to do was open her legs a bit for his cock to slide between them. Her ass was firm and massaged him nicely as she and Slocum ground against each other. When he squeezed her breasts, she pulled in a deep breath, and when he pinched her nipples, she had to fight against squealing with delight.

"What's the matter?" he whispered. "Don't want to make too much noise?"

"I . . . am still working, you know," she said in a voice that was colored by more of a Mexican accent than when she was fully composed.

"So the management frowns on this sort of thing?"

"I'd rather not find out."

Slocum put his hands back onto her hips and pushed her forward a few steps. From the moment he'd seen the spark that had been in her eyes when he'd signed the Dodge House's register, he knew this moment would come. Now that it was here, he positioned her in front of another bathtub and eased his cock between her thighs. She bent forward, grabbed on to the edge of the tub, and moved her feet apart to spread her legs for him. That way, he could enter her from behind while she held on to maintain her balance.

The instant Slocum found the lips of her pussy, he could feel her body tense. She was even wetter there than the rest of her body, which still dripped with hot water. Now that he was closer to her, he could smell the scented salts she must have put into the bath. That, along with the natural scent of her body, drifted through the air as he started pumping. Estrella grunted every time he thrust into her. When Slocum found his rhythm, she tossed her head back to send her black hair over her shoulders.

Slocum looked down to admire the curve of her hips and the slope of her back. Her hair was wet and clung to her in ropy strands. He savored the feel of her body wriggling between his palms as every inch of his cock glided in and out of her. When the mood struck him, he gripped her tighter and pounded into her harder. Estrella arched her shoulders and braced her legs to receive him.

"Dios mio," she cried. *"Delo a mi."*

She was begging for him to give it to her, and hearing the request in Spanish made Slocum want to honor it even more. Every time he drove into her, Estrella's entire body trembled. Soon, the sound of their bodies coming together filled the room along with the moans that she tried so desperately to stifle. When Slocum pulled out of her, she let go of a breath as if she'd been holding it for days. Estrella spun around and came at him with fire in her eyes. Her hands pressed against his chest at the same time her lips pressed against his mouth. When Slocum once more grabbed her hips, she began gnawing impatiently on the side of his neck.

Before he could decide where to take her next, she pushed him with the same amount of urgency that he'd shown when getting her to the side of the tub. Estrella moved him to a high-backed chair that sat in the corner of the largest stall. It was padded with soft white cushions that felt good against his body as he allowed himself to drop down onto the decorative furniture. The moment he was settled, Estrella climbed on top of him to straddle his hips.

She spoke in a steady torrent of Spanish promises regarding what she intended on doing to him. Her voice was harsh and musky, reaching down to a primal part of him that was stimulated even more by the touch of her hand along the shaft of his cock. He felt his tip brush against her damp pussy before she lowered herself down onto him. From there, she wasted no time whatsoever before bracing her hands against his chest and riding him in a furious bucking motion.

"Damn, girl," Slocum said as he tried to steady her. "You're about to break this fancy chair!"

But Estrella didn't care about that. She was completely absorbed in the act of riding him and probably couldn't even hear what he said above the sound of her own voice. She closed her eyes and dug her fingernails into Slocum's flesh while arching her back.

Since he wasn't about to try and slow her down, Slocum cupped her backside in both hands and pounded his cock up into her. After just a few powerful thrusts, she leaned forward to place her hands upon the back of the chair on either side of Slocum's head. That placed her close enough for him to kiss and lick the smooth slopes of her breasts while continuing to pump between her thighs.

Sweat mingled with the scented water beading upon her skin when she slowed down to a gentle rocking pace. Estrella looked down at him and said, "I wanted you inside me the first night you checked in."

"You should've said something."

"So should you."

"Actions speak louder than words."

"That is why I met you here today," she said.

Slocum locked eyes with her, ran his hands along her thighs, and drove into her with solid, powerful movements. She grunted softly with each impact, placing her hands upon her breasts and rubbing herself as she was brought toward climax. Slocum could feel her pussy tightening around him and could see the expression on her face shifting as she gave herself over to the pleasure coursing through her body. As her groans became louder, he felt the tide within him start to build. She had to purse her lips shut tightly when he exploded inside her, barely maintaining enough control to keep from filling the bathroom with her passionate cries.

After taking a few seconds to catch her breath, Estrella climbed off him and went to the bathtub. "Your water is still warm," she said while dipping her hand in to splash some of it onto her chest and neck.

"Considering how bad everyone thinks I smell, I'm surprised you were able to get so close to me."

"I like a man to smell like a man. You are like a wild animal between my legs."

"Somehow I thought you might say something like that." Slocum stood up and made his way to the only tub that had been filled. "Still, it's high time for me to clean up."

"I agree. Sometimes being like an animal is good. Other times . . . not so good."

She stood in front of him, dripping and naked. Slocum wrapped his arms around her and kissed her on the lips. After a few short seconds, he felt his body once more responding to her warmth. Estrella pulled away and picked up a nearby towel. "Don't start something we can't finish."

"Oh, I can finish it all right."

"But I can't. If I don't show my face downstairs soon, people will think I left early for the day. Not all of us can come and go as they please, you know."

"I suppose being a transient does have its advantages," Slocum chuckled.

Having mostly dried herself, Estrella turned to look at him while holding the towel against her breasts. "What was that?"

"Nothing," Slocum said as he eased into the water. "Do whatever you need to do."

All Estrella needed to do was get dressed and primp herself so it wasn't too obvious what she'd been doing for the last several minutes. Slocum admired the view while settling his back against the rounded surface of the bathtub. In no time at all, she was ready to face the rest of the Dodge

House. Estrella unlocked the door, peeked outside, and gave him a quick wave before ducking out and shutting the door behind her.

Slocum grinned wider than the cat that ate the canary. The water was still hot and did wonders to soothe his tired muscles. Soap cut through the dirt that had caked onto his skin, leaving him smelling more like a human being and less like a dog that had spent the last week and a half sleeping in a ditch.

5

The rest of the day went by so well that it was easy for Slocum to forget about what he had planned for the evening. After changing into his fresher set of clothes, he dropped the old ones off at the Dodge House's laundry. The man working behind the counter there stood as if he had starch running through his veins and couldn't guarantee that the clothes would only need to be run through once. Slocum left them in his hands and headed back to Anne's stable. After cleaning out the stalls and moving several bales of hay, he still didn't stink as bad as he had earlier that morning.

When he returned to the front desk of the Dodge House, Slocum was greeted by a sly, knowing grin on the face of the younger girl who'd greeted him earlier. "I hear you had a very nice bath," she said.

"Word travels fast, huh?"

"Yes, but not too far. Me and Estrella talk a lot and she had nothing but good things to say about you. Nothing too personal, though. Just good." Judging by the curl of her lips and the flush in her cheeks, that last little statement was a long ways from the truth.

"Can you do me a favor?"

Thoroughly enjoying the way Slocum leaned on the edge of the desk and lowered his voice as if he had a secret to share, the girl nodded and replied, "Of course, Mr. Slocum."

"I'd like to reserve a room for a friend of mine. Is there any way I can put his name down so he'll be sure to have one when he arrives?"

She nodded enthusiastically. "I can take a reservation. What's his name?"

"George Myer."

"When will he be arriving?"

"Should be any time. Here's the thing, though. If anyone asks, I'd like you to tell them that Mr. Myer is already here."

"What? Why would you want me to do that?"

"It's a surprise."

Slocum gambled on that being enough to both pique the girl's interest and discourage her from pressing the matter any further. Since she already had a few juicy secrets where he was concerned, she didn't seem to mind being entrusted with another. As if demonstrating her willingness to keep her mouth shut on the matter, she turned the register around and printed *George Myer—rm. 49* on the next empty line. When she turned the register back to face the customer's side of the desk, she was showing him her familiar little smirk.

"Much obliged," Slocum told her with a quick wink.

He checked in at the laundry and wasn't surprised when he was asked to approve that his clothes be put through another round of cleaning. After that, Slocum decided to have a look at Room 49. It was near the end of the hall at the opposite side of the building from his own room. When he went to the room and knocked on the door, it was answered within a few seconds by an older woman who wore a simple brown dress and her hair tied back by a matching kerchief. "Yes?" she said.

"Pardon me. Are you renting this room?"

"No. Just cleaning it."

"Mind if I take a quick look inside?"

She blinked, looked over her shoulder, and then back to him. "Why would you want to do that?"

Fortunately, Slocum's head was clear enough to come up with something quickly. "I was thinking about asking for another room and wanted to see if they're all the same."

"Was your other one dirty? Was something wrong?"

Noticing the insulted tone in her voice as well as the glint in her eyes, Slocum replied, "No, nothing like that. It's the bed and window. They both seem so small and I wanted to see if it was worth changing rooms or if it's just me being too big for my own damn good."

Slocum wasn't an overly large man, but the maid had apparently heard much stranger complaints. Since his problem didn't seem to have to do with anything that fell within her responsibilities, she shrugged and stepped aside. "I suppose you could take a quick look while I finish up."

"Much obliged," Slocum said with a tip of his hat. Unlike the younger girl behind the front desk, this woman wasn't impressed by the mediocre display of civility.

Inside, the room was identical to number 42. He wasn't at all interested in the size of the bed, but he walked over to it and hunkered down for a closer look just to keep up the guise of why he was in the room. The maid watched him like a hawk. She tensed when he stretched out his arms so he could take a measurement in a fashion similar to an undertaker getting the feel for what size coffin was needed to bury a particularly big corpse. When he stood up and walked toward the window, the maid swooped in to fix the sheet and blanket even though he hadn't actually touched either of them.

What Slocum really wanted to see was the view from the window. He chuckled to himself just because asking for that specifically would have been a better excuse to step into the room than the one he'd given. The maid was still wrapping up her chores, however, and didn't seem to care what he was doing so long as it didn't create a mess. Slocum glanced out through the freshly cleaned glass to get a view of the corner of Railroad and Front Streets. Railroad led down to a clear stretch compared to the bustle that was almost always found on Front.

"You through, mister?" the maid asked.

"I am."

"Then out with you. If you like the room, tell it to the front desk."

"I will. Thanks for your time."

She shooed him out, locked up, and started in on Room 50.

By the time Slocum returned to the Dodge House Saloon, it was about an hour before the restaurant's dinner rush. Everett was behind the bar, wearing a shirt that was so damp he must have been sweating bullets for hours on end. When he saw Slocum approach, he practically hopped over the bar in his haste to greet him. Slocum saved him the trouble and approached to order a beer.

"Milt already stopped by," Everett said while placing a frothy mug on the bar.

"Good. What did you tell him?"

"I said there might be some worthwhile prospects coming by later tonight. I didn't know what else to tell him because you never mentioned what I should say. All you said was that I should wait for you to arrive and you didn't arrive until now."

Slocum had to fight to keep from laughing at the way Everett's words spilled out of him. "Take a breath," he said after sipping his beer. "In fact, have a beer. It's pretty good."

"Yeah, that's what you drank the night you staggered out of here."

"Hmm," Slocum said while examining the mug as if it could tell him anything else about his behavior that fateful night. Since he'd already pieced together what he needed to know, he took another sip and set the mug down. "When are they coming back?"

"Could be any second. If they see me talking to you, this whole damn thing could be blown."

"What whole thing? You don't even know what it is yet. And as for me talking to you, I'm staying at this hotel. They must've already known that much."

Everett pulled in a deep breath, held it, and nodded. "You're right. Thanks."

"Don't get all grateful just yet. You still have to answer for setting me up. I want you to tell Milt or Fitz that I'm looking for them."

"They're not hard to find."

Slocum glared at the bartender until the other man started to squirm. Once he knew he wasn't about to be interrupted again, he said, "I realize that, but I want you to tell them anyway. Make sure to let them know I'm still fired up about what they did and that I'll be looking to take a piece out of every one of them. I want them dead, you understand? Dead after bleeding out like a couple of fucking dogs for God and everyone else in Dodge City to see."

Everett nodded solemnly as if the threat had been levied directly at him.

"If they're still interested in any other news of the usual sort they're after, tell them there's a rich fellow by the name of George Myer staying at the hotel here."

"Who is he?"

"Myer is in Dodge on business involving a large sum of money. Since he's going to be leaving tomorrow, he's keeping the money in his room instead of bothering with a bank. The deal is happening around midnight, so he'll be gone before then and returning to collect it."

"What kind of business?"

"Does that really matter?"

Everett thought that over for much too long before shaking his head and muttering, "I suppose it don't. Midnight, you say?"

"That's right. You heard about all of this from the only armed guard accompanying Myer on his ride through town. If anyone asks where the guard is, say he's in the company of a working girl down the street."

"Probably Tammy's, I reckon."

At that moment, Slocum honestly couldn't tell whether or not Everett knew he was being told a story that wasn't true. Seeing as how that issue may only confuse the bartender, he nodded and said, "I reckon so."

Beaming like a schoolboy who'd guessed the right answer to an arithmetic problem, Everett seemed more at ease than at any other point since Slocum had known him. "I'll do that, Mr. Slocum."

"Tell me what you're going to say, Everett."

"That you're looking for them. Want to kill them like dogs and all of that. Also that there's a fella by the name of George Myer staying at the hotel with a bag of money sitting up in his room on account of some business deal. He's got an armed man with him to watch over the cash, but he's off with some whore at Tammy's down the street. The money should be in the room until midnight or so, which is when the Myer fella said his business would be over. Or maybe it was the guard who said that. Which was it again?"

Slocum tipped back his beer and set it down. "You got it right just the way it is. What will you say if they ask where you heard about Myer?"

"I'll just tell him it was my usual sources. That's always been good enough before, and there ain't no reason it wouldn't be good enough now. In fact, I'll let him know that the news about Myer is why I came along to work tonight instead of during my normal hours! A cut from a job that juicy would be a sight to see."

"It's gonna square things up between you and me, so you're getting plenty out of this deal."

Everett's mood darkened as he was reminded of what had gotten the ruse started in the first place. By the time he'd collected Slocum's mug and wiped off the wet circle left behind on the bar, he seemed just as rattled as when the conversation had begun. "I'll do what you asked, Mr. Slocum."

For some reason, Slocum found himself feeling bad for all but knocking the joy from the bartender's face. He'd crossed paths with plenty of bad men and even more yellow-bellied assholes who would sell their mother's soul for a few dollars. Everett may have been greasy, but he didn't exactly strike Slocum as either of those kinds of men. Because of that, he asked, "Can you tell me one more thing?"

"Depends on what it is."

"You seem like an amicable sort. Why would you get mixed up with the likes of Cameron or those other two?"

"The money," he replied with shame in his voice. "Whenever I give them a tip that pans out, I get a cut of their take. If it wasn't for all of my debts, I wouldn't even bother."

"That's over, though, right?"

"Yes, sir," Everett replied. "I remember what I told you before. That's behind me now. And if it makes you feel any better, I didn't get a cut of anything that night they met you in Tin Pot Alley."

Without hesitation, Slocum replied, "It doesn't."

6

Slocum spent the better part of that night in his room. Although he hadn't told anyone he'd be up there, he made sure to order enough food and drink from room service that anyone who asked around even halfheartedly would know where to find him. He ate the sandwiches and drank the water that was brought to him while whiling away the hours playing solitaire.

Every time a set of footsteps thumped down the hall, he went to his door and listened. So far, he'd only heard the voices of couples going to their rooms to be alone or solitary guests unlocking one of the other rooms on that floor. Slocum was keenly aware of the weight of the .38 at his hip. When he hadn't been amusing himself playing cards, he'd stripped the pistol down, put it back together, unloaded it, and then reloaded it with the ammunition he'd bought at a store down the street. The gun had seen plenty of use and was in fine condition, which meant Milt would be anxious to get it back. As noise from the first floor of the Dodge House grew louder and more boisterous, Slocum knew he wouldn't have to wait long for the gun's previous owner to make good on that desire.

When Slocum felt boredom taking too deep of a hold or his eyes drooping too far down, he stood up and moved around to get his blood flowing. Every so often, a splash of water on his face brought his senses back to where they needed to be.

Finally, he heard the footsteps he'd been waiting for.

It was just past ten thirty at night and the saloon had yet to reach its rowdiest point. The steps that thumped down the hall were quick, but not rushed. They had weight to them, but didn't sound heavy. Whoever was walking wasn't exactly sneaking, but they weren't announcing their presence either. Most important, Slocum's gut told him they were definite prospects for belonging to the men he was after. It had been long enough for Cameron, Milt, and Fitz to have arrived and gotten settled. Surely, Milt would have spoken with Everett by now and the story had been passed along. There had even been enough time for one of those hired gunmen to come up with the idea of going to the hotel's front desk and checking the register to verify that George Myer was a guest and that he was staying in Room 49. Slocum smiled to himself and drew his pistol. Sometimes, there simply wasn't a joy in the world to compare with watching pieces of a plan fit together like well-oiled gears.

He placed his back against the wall to the left of his room's door. The .38 was kept in a low grip and his ear was placed against the wall. Slocum closed his eyes and even held his breath so he could hear as much as possible as those footsteps moved toward his room from the direction of the stairs. There was obviously more than one person clomping past his door. Judging by the weight behind their steps, both were grown men.

Slocum reached for the door handle, waited for the steps to pass, and then opened it a fraction of an inch. He waited

with his ear close to the crack he'd created just in case anyone outside noticed the slight movement from his door. Since
the steps didn't break their stride, he was confident he hadn't
been spotted. Even so, he waited for them to reach the end
of the hall before making his move.

Another door farther down the hall was shaken on its
hinges as the men who'd walked by tested the strength of
its lock. Slocum wanted to peek out and see which door they
were at, but stopped short. If they were facing a door on
either side of the hall, there was a better chance of them
noticing movement from the corners of their eyes. More
important, if they were trying to force their way into what
they thought was another person's room, they would most
likely be looking around to see if anyone was watching them
from anywhere along the hall. If those two men were Milt
and Fitz, they also probably knew which room was Slocum's
and could be glancing toward his door at this moment.

Ignoring the impulse coming from damn near every bone
in his body, Slocum remained still. From a distance, he
hoped his door would look like all the others along the hallway despite the fact that it was slightly ajar.

The movement down the hall stopped.

If Slocum strained his ears, he thought he could hear
hushed voices coming from that direction.

Before he had a chance to wonder what the two men were
talking about, he heard the creak of hinges and the shuffle
of hurried steps. Slocum grinned and waited for a few seconds before making another move. Once he was fairly certain the men at the other end of the hall had gotten enough
time to cross a threshold, he pulled the door open. He'd
hoped to catch a glimpse of which door had been opened
down the hall before it was closed again. What he didn't
expect to see was a slender man standing directly in front
of his door with one hand reaching for the handle.

The man was half an inch shorter than Slocum and had
a lean build. Sunken cheeks and a pointed chin were

accented by a thin, neatly trimmed mustache and a narrow patch of whiskers running down from his lower lip. His eyes were dark and focused upon the door's handle, but snapped up toward Slocum in a flicker of barely perceptible motion. It took less than a heartbeat for Slocum to overcome his initial surprise. Unfortunately, the slender man standing in front of him reacted just as quickly.

As Slocum reached out to pull the man into his room, the wiry visitor lunged forward. Apparently, they both had the same idea of clearing the hallway before being spotted. Since the other man was so much lighter than he, all Slocum needed to do was step back with one foot and twist sideways to allow him to bounce off him and stumble inside. From there, he took a quick peek down the hall to see that all the other doors were closed and then shut the one to his room.

"Who the hell are you?" Slocum asked.

Although the man had entered in a less than graceful manner, he'd recovered his balance quickly and put his back to a wall. Narrow eyes darted toward Slocum's holster and back up again. When Slocum's hand shifted, the man rushed forward with surprising speed. Before Slocum could get a grip on the .38, the other man had reached out to grab his wrist and twist it painfully against its joint.

Rather than fight against the hold that had ensnared his arm, Slocum shifted to keep his wrist from being broken and turned his entire body around while dropping one shoulder. The other man was lifted off his feet to be carried over Slocum's hip. After rolling like rain off Slocum's back, the man hit the floor on both feet and pulled his arm free to snap a few quick jabs to his ribs. The blows didn't hurt, but they robbed Slocum of just enough breath to slow him down.

Slocum's next backhanded swing sliced through empty air, missing the other man's chin by an inch or two. When the other man leaned forward after dodging the blow, he reached for a scabbard tied to his right leg by two leather cords. "I didn't come here to fight," he said.

"You're the one that shoved into my room!" Slocum pointed out.

"I was just going to knock on your door."

Not liking the fact that the other man still hadn't taken his hand away from his scabbard, Slocum slipped his fingers around the .38's grip. The instant his finger touched the trigger, the other man drew his knife and cocked it back near his right ear. The blade was as skinny as the man who held it.

"I can bring this to a quick end as well, you know," the other man warned. Since the blade looked to be balanced for throwing and his entire body was coiled like a spring, the threat was anything but empty.

For the next few seconds, neither man said anything. When a thump sounded from farther down the hall, both of them glanced toward it. Something in Slocum's gut told him the other man's reaction stemmed from something other than basic reflex or curiosity.

"You didn't want to be seen by whoever was walking down that hall in front of you," Slocum said.

Without hesitation, the other man replied, "And neither did you."

"Who are you? Do you work for Cameron?"

"No."

"What about Milt?"

That name brought a visceral reaction to the other man that was equal parts anger and disgust. "I sure as hell don't work for that son of a bitch!"

"But you know him." Slocum's muscles may have relaxed somewhat, but they didn't allow his hand to stray too far from his holstered pistol. "And it seems you don't hold him in any higher regard than I do."

The other man's face twitched, but the knife in his hand remained still. "Take your hand away from that pistol," he said.

"Put your knife away first."

The other man lowered his knife until it hung just above

the opening of its scabbard. That didn't make things overly friendly between the men since all it would take was a flick of the man's wrist to toss the blade into Slocum's belly.

As a way of furthering the prospect of goodwill, Slocum peeled his fingers away from the .38 and lifted his hand an inch above the gun. Like the other man's situation, he would only need to make a single quick move to defend himself if the need should arise.

After sizing Slocum up one last time, the man eased the knife into its scabbard and allowed his hands to hang at his sides. "My name's Daniel Garner."

"John Slocum," he said while taking a similar casual yet cautious stance.

"I know who you are, Mr. Slocum."

"All right then. The next question is why you decided to storm into my room. And don't tell me it's because I dragged you in. We both know damn well you were headed this direction no matter what I meant to do."

"I was asking around about where I might find Milton Connoway and was told you were looking for him as well. Milton and another fellow walked right by me when I was coming to your room, and it was all I could do to keep from being seen. I don't know how long they intend on staying up here, but we may not have a lot of time to catch up to them."

"How do you know Milt?"

"There ain't time to tell that story right now. He's a slippery bastard and I don't want to take the chance of losing him again. The only reason I came to your room was to see if you might know how many men he's got working for him here in Dodge."

"From what I've seen, he and one other man are on another man's payroll." Slocum stopped talking when he heard more shuffling footsteps from the end of the hall. They were too light and coming from the wrong direction to be the ones he'd heard before. "Did you get a look at who Milt was with?"

"Some smaller dude who looked like he got a haircut from a machete."

"That'd be Fitz. Him and Milt are working for a gambler named Cameron. Do any of those names ring a bell?"

Daniel didn't have to think for long before shaking his head. "No, but Milt's worked with plenty of men. You're staying at this hotel. Do you know if he meets up with any other rough sorts here?"

"I already told you that."

"You told me about a gambler." Daniel waved a frustrated hand at Slocum and turned toward the door as if he'd suddenly grown tired of looking at him. "I wasted too much time already."

"So you're sure that was Milt who walked down the hall before you?"

"There ain't no way I'd miss that one."

"Did he go to Room 49?"

"The one at the end of the hall," Daniel replied.

"Then he won't be in there for long. I arranged for him to go to that room as a way for me to get the drop on him. Now, thanks to you, I already lost that advantage."

"I was thinking the same thing."

Before their aggravated banter could continue, Slocum and Daniel were drawn to the sound of a door being swung open to pound against a wall. It came from the end of the hall they'd both been watching and the voices that followed were anything but amused.

"Sounds like them right now," Slocum said. "If you're out to ruin Milt's night, then we might as well work together."

"Fine, but if things get rough, just stay out of my way."

Although Daniel was closer to the door and able to pull it open, Slocum was the first one to storm into the hall. At the far end, standing directly in front of Room 49, were Milt and Fitz. Both men already had their guns drawn and took a moment to see who'd come out to join them. When he saw Slocum's face, Milt shouted, "There you are, John! Thought you would've hightailed it out of town by now."

Slocum wasn't about to engage in any more small talk. Instead, he ran down the hall like a bull charging a fluttering red cape.

Milt sighted along the top of his gun while Fitz ducked back into Room 49 and poked his head out to take aim.

Without slowing his charge, Slocum brought the .38 from its holster and fired in a lightning-fast series of movements. His first shot was wild and he knew it wouldn't draw any blood as it thundered down the hall. Even so, the chunk of hot lead threw off the other two gunmen's aim as it chewed into the wall within a few inches of their heads. Milt shoved his way back into Room 49 and Slocum fired one more shot to convince them to stay put until he could get there. Just as he arrived and before he could fire again, something leapt at him through the doorway like a cat that had been waiting to pounce from a corner.

It was Fitz. The smaller man had his gun in one hand and a hunting knife in the other. Slocum could see as much because both weapons passed directly in front of his face as Fitz attacked. He leaned back to let a slash from the knife pass by just close enough to open a shallow gash in his cheek. Slocum brought the .38 around to jam the barrel into Fitz's ribs for an easy shot, but the knife was already coming back to swing at that arm. Although he retracted his arm before his wrist was cut open, Slocum wasn't able to take a shot. Instead, he delivered a chopping uppercut to Fitz's stomach and followed up with a blow using the side of the .38.

"You're dead!" Fitz snarled as he leaned in to put some more of his weight behind his blade.

Slocum's pistol glanced off Fitz's shoulder. Even when

he was tangled up and struggling to stay alive, Fitz was a wiry cuss who avoided taking enough damage to put him down. The blade sliced out toward Slocum's gun hand one more time. If the swing was only intended to prevent him from taking aim at point-blank range, it had succeeded beautifully. No matter how close he was to his target, trying to use the .38 now was as good an idea as sticking his hand into a wildcat's mouth. He brought his knee up into Fitz's body, but felt the smaller man twist so he could all but conform to Slocum's leg.

Suddenly, Fitz was torn away from Slocum. The gunman screeched loudly while swinging his blade. This time, however, Fitz's hunting knife scraped against another blade to send a shower of sparks through the air. Not only had Daniel been the one to pull Fitz away, but he'd also been quick enough to raise his own knife to deflect the incoming blow.

"The room's empty!" Slocum shouted once he'd fully disentangled himself from Fitz and gotten a look through the door. "Milt must've gone out the window."

"Give me a second," Daniel said as he launched Fitz into the closest wall. "I'll come with you."

Slocum was already stomping through Room 49 and taking a quick look around to make certain the open window wasn't just a diversion. Having seen the room when it had been straightened not too long ago, Slocum could tell that the bed and the rest of the furniture hadn't been disturbed. If a man of Milt's size was trying to hide somewhere in such a quick amount of time, he would have needed to be part chameleon.

"I'm going after him," Slocum announced. "Soon as you can, circle around outside and meet up with us. We'll probably be heading down Railroad."

Daniel was struggling with Fitz, but landing some pretty solid blows when he asked, "How the hell do you know that much?"

"Because I scouted it out. You can trust me or not, but

I'm not about to let this son of a bitch get away." Without waiting for another word from the hall, Slocum stuck his head out the window and looked outside.

There was a fair amount of commotion on the streets below, but the people down Railroad Street moved more like ripples left behind after a rock had been tossed into a pond. Relying on the information he'd put together earlier, Slocum followed his instincts and climbed out onto the over-hang of the roof that provided a lip around the building between the top two floors. For once, Slocum wished that someone would have taken a shot at him. At least that way he would know for certain he was going the right direction. But Milt either was too busy running or unwilling to tip his hand. Slocum skidded along the edge of the roof until he found an awning that was just between him and street level. He lowered himself down and dropped onto the wooden awning. The structure was more than strong enough to sup-port his weight, and according to the fresh scuff marks along its surface, another man had followed that exact route not too long ago. With the scent of his prey fresh in his nose, Slocum jumped down to street level and started running.

Although he may have picked the correct direction at the start, Slocum quickly realized there was no way of knowing where to go from there. Railroad wasn't as crowded or noisy as Front Street, but there was no shortage of alleys, doorways, or dark corners for a man to choose from if he was looking to quickly get out of sight. Before Slocum could lose hope, a series of raised voices came from farther down the street.

"Watch where you're headed!" one of them shouted.

There was some commotion, possibly from a struggle, followed by a more familiar voice that said, "Step aside, *now!*"

Slocum didn't bother with any attempt at stealth as he raced toward the voices. He was about five paces in front of a narrow alleyway when a pair of cowboys stepped out. They were riled up and eager to meet Slocum head-on. Rather than start another fight, Slocum asked, "Did a man about my size with long hair come through here?"

The taller of the two other men wore a large hat that was pulled down tightly to remain in place against the will of persistent prairie winds. He stepped aside, hooked a thumb over his shoulder, and said, "Just passed him. Seemed ready for a fight, though."

"He's about to get one."

Slocum may not have been able to see the two cowboys once he was running down the alley, but he could hear the older one just fine when he shouted, "Split that rude bastard's lip open, mister!"

The lanterns illuminating a few of the storefronts as well as the street itself weren't very bright, but their light was brilliant compared to the gloom in that alley. Slocum did his best to tread as carefully as possible while allowing his eyes to adjust. He could hear Milt's frenzied steps ahead and got a real good look at him the second Milt emerged from the opposite end of the alley to check which way he should go next.

Immediately after Slocum set his sights on the fleeing thief, Milt spun around and raised his gun. "That you, Slocum?" he asked while firing a wild shot into the alley. "I got somethin' for ya!"

Now Slocum was the one who had the advantage of being in the shadows. Rather than return fire right away, Slocum slowed down so he could position himself against one of the encroaching buildings. Everything from Milt's meandering eyes to his irregular line of fire made it clear that he couldn't see his target.

"You hidin', Slocum? From what I heard about you, I wouldn't expect you to squat in the dark pissin' yourself in fear."

Even though Slocum knew damn well that Milt was just trying to bait him into coming out so he could get his head blown off, those words still made him want to break from cover just to shut Milt's fat mouth for good.

But Slocum didn't have to.

Suddenly, silently, a figure lunged in the darkness and pounced on Milt. That silent movement more than the shape of the figure that had jumped from out of nowhere let Slocum know who it was.

"What in the hell?" Milt squawked as he was brought down to the ground. Daniel dragged him down and had straddled his chest to rain a series of furious blows down on him, but Milt still couldn't get a good enough look at his attacker to decide if he was man or beast.

Daniel was still swinging and landing several punches that caught Milt in the face and neck. It wasn't much longer before Milt collected himself enough to remember the gun in his hand. He brought the .44 up, but suddenly found his gun arm moving the wrong direction when Slocum pinned that hand down by stepping on his wrist.

"Get this son of a bitch offa me!" Milt screamed.

Slocum winced as one powerful punch cracked against Milt's jaw and snapped his head to one side. "Sure," he said while watching Daniel beat Milt some more. "Just as soon as I stop pissing myself in fear."

7

Daniel had rented a small room in the Lady Gay farther down Front Street. Since it was a little ways from the Dodge House and Daniel already knew two different ways to get there without being spotted, Slocum agreed to bring Milt there. Needless to say, the gunman wasn't at all happy with the arrangement. He kicked and struggled every step of the way, which didn't make much of a dent in the commotion already filling Dodge City's saloon district at that time of night. Now that the gunfire had died down, the local law wasn't in a hurry to investigate Milt's loud complaints. In fact, as the gunman was escorted across the street, a few drunks chimed in as if Milt were merely wailing another off-key melody.

"Might as well settle down, big man," Slocum said while slapping Milt on the back. "You're only making a fool out of yourself."

"You think so?" Milt growled as he wheeled around. "Untie my hands and we'll see who the fool is." When Slocum didn't immediately rise to the challenge, Milt let out a single humorless laugh. "That's right. Just like I thought."

They were within a few steps of the narrow stairs that led up to the second floor of the Lady Gay Saloon. Slocum had tied a rope around Milt's wrists with enough slack for Daniel to lead him along like a dog on a leash. Daniel tugged on the rope to drag Milt toward the stairs, and Milt seemed more than happy to go along after having said his piece.

Slocum grabbed Milt's shoulder, spun him around, and glared directly into his eyes. "You really don't know when to shut your mouth, do you?"

Milt looked at him without saying a word, but the smug grin on his face spoke volumes.

"Come on," Daniel urged. "We can't finish our business out in the open. This one's friends might be looking for him."

"Oh, they'll be looking, all right," Milt said. "That is, unless you killed Fitz to keep him from talking." He glanced over at Daniel for all of two seconds before chuckling, "Nah. You don't have it in you to do that."

"Don't be so sure," Daniel warned.

Milt shrugged and turned toward the stairs. "You boys gonna get on with this or not? I got things to do."

"What makes you think you'll be doing anything after tonight?" Daniel asked.

"Because if you were gonna do more than talk tough, you would'a done it by now."

Slocum grabbed Milt's shoulder once again while drawing the slender-bladed knife from his right boot to cut the ropes binding Milt's wrists. A few drops of blood spilled when Milt's hands came loose, but he didn't have any time to think about that before Slocum said, "You want a chance to prove yourself? You got it."

Daniel positioned himself so he was out of Milt's reach as he placed his hand upon the grip of his holstered pistol. "Enough of this. We need to get him upstairs and out of sight."

"Best listen to your little friend, Johnny," Milt warned.

"Don't worry about him," Slocum replied. "You've got enough on your plate worrying about me."

Milt kept the tough act going for a few more seconds. He even puffed out his chest as if he was actually going to take a run at Slocum. When Slocum grinned as though eagerly awaiting another chance to spill some of Milt's blood, the captured gunman lost some of his steam.

"What's wrong?" Slocum asked. "Didn't expect me to call your bluff?"

"Wasn't a bluff," Milt spat. "I just ain't stupid enough to take a run at an armed man."

Slocum nodded and used his free hand to lift the .38 from his holster and let it drop. "There you go. Feel better?" When Milt silently ground his teeth and shifted from one foot to another, Slocum grabbed his hand in a spot where he was sure to press his finger against the fresh cut in Milt's wrist. After flipping his knife around and placing its handle on Milt's palm, Slocum took a step back and opened his arms. "How's that? Feeling braver now?"

Milt's hand tightened around the knife's handle. His eyes narrowed and his mouth became a thin, severe line.

Daniel maintained his position and said, "This is—"

"Shut up," Slocum barked. "This asshole's done nothing but talk tough and shoot when he's got the upper hand. The only thing that shows less backbone than that is bushwhacking another man from behind and emptying his pockets. Wait a second. He's done that, too."

Milt twitched at that, but couldn't dispute the claim.

Taking half a step closer, Slocum stared into Milt's eyes while keeping the gunman's hands within the lower periphery of his field of vision. "See, that's the problem with flapping your gums so much. Sooner or later, someone gets tired of listening and you gotta be ready to back yourself up."

"I make a move," Milt grumbled, "and that little fella behind me puts me down."

"Not before I do," Slocum said. "I promise you that."

There was no arguing with the deadly vow etched into Slocum's hardened features. Milt did his best to keep his chin up, but soon his head became too heavy to hold up and it drooped in silent defeat. His fingers relaxed, allowing the knife to slip from them before he brought his wrists together as if they were once again bound by a length of rope. "Whatever you got in mind, let's just get it over with."

Having already made his point, Slocum waited for Milt to walk away before scooping up the knife and pistol. Even as he did so, he half expected Milt to seize the chance to jump on him. If that happened, Slocum was prepared to drive his fist into Milt's gut and snap his neck like a chicken's. Once again, to Slocum's dismay, Milt didn't give him the opportunity for payback.

Daniel shoved Milt in front of him so they could climb up to the second floor. At the top of the stairs, a door opened into the end of a hallway that looked like a smaller version of the one in the Dodge House Hotel. Then again, it didn't take much for hotels to start looking alike to Slocum.

"Have a seat," Daniel said after unlocking a door and shoving Milt toward a chair that had already been set up in the middle of the floor next to a narrow bed and a little dresser with a chipped washbasin on it.

Milt did as he was told, huffing loudly as if the weight of the world rested upon his shoulders.

The room was clean and sparsely furnished. Slocum followed the other two men inside and glanced down the hallway to check the path that led to the stairs as well as the other direction, which led to an open staircase echoing with noise and music from the saloon below. Unlike the finery of the Dodge House, the rooms at the Lady Gay appeared to be either an afterthought or a place for the working girls to ply their trade. Since nobody was poking their noses out to check on them and nobody had been interested enough to follow them from the street, Slocum shut the door and locked it.

Daniel looped the rope around Milt's chest and quickly knotted it behind the back of the chair to hold the gunman down. "You know who I am?" he asked.

Still feeling the sting from being put in his place downstairs, Milt kept his head hanging low and grumbled, "How the fuck should I know?"

Even Slocum was surprised when Daniel reached out with one hand to slap the side of Milt's head with enough force to rattle whatever brains were in his skull. "What about Misty Creek?" Daniel asked. "That sound familiar?"

Milt's eyes snapped open and darted back and forth before he closed them tightly again. The silence that fell over him after that was thicker than the sweat pasting his shirt to his back.

"What's Misty Creek?" Slocum asked.

Milt kept his head hanging low and Daniel seemed too angry to form a sentence.

"You know the answer to that," Slocum said as he reached out to grab Milt's chin so he could stare into the gunman's eyes. Since this was the second time he'd been cowed into silence, Milt was held upright mainly by the rope tying him to the chair. "You know the answer," Slocum roared. "Tell me!"

"It's just some piss hole a few days north of here," Milt replied.

When he exhaled, Slocum felt the last few nights rush to catch up with him. His head still ached from where he'd been hit. His cheek still ached from where it had been cut. His legs were sore from so much running. His ears jangled with the noise of gunshots and shouting. When he allowed Milt's head to hang forward, he found himself envying the gunman for being able to sit and not think about much of anything. Looking to Daniel, he asked, "What's Misty Creek?"

"It's a trickle of water running from southwest Nebraska to cut through the northern corner of Kansas," Daniel said. Now that Milt was tied up and uninterested in making another move, Daniel walked over to the window, which was covered by a set of dark red curtains. Holding some of the curtains aside, he gazed down at the street. "It's not big enough to be considered a trade route, but it provides irrigation to a farm or two. The Pawnee are thick in those parts as well. Least, they used to be."

"Fucking Injuns ain't nothing but bugs anyhow," Milt said.

Shifting his gaze toward Milt as if he'd just discovered a dead skunk under his bed, Daniel continued, "Up until a few weeks ago, I was a scout for a Cavalry Division stationed in Nebraska. We rode the trails through there to look for any ranchers or covered wagons that may have gotten robbed or otherwise accosted along their way. As you probably know, Indians can be a problem in that respect."

"Yeah," Slocum said. "I know."

"If Indians become too much of a problem, it's the Army's duty to bring them to justice. That usually gets bloody. Well, somewhere near the end of last winter, a stretch of trails got hit pretty hard and folks were turning up dead. I was with a unit that found one wagon train torn up so bad, it would've made the devil's stomach turn. Men were gutted like fish. Women and children were laying in the dirt with their . . . well . . . it was a sight that'd rattle anyone."

"Just like I said," Milt grumbled. "Nothin' but bugs."

Daniel stared at the gunman with such intensity that Slocum began to wonder if he might be forced to step in to keep Daniel from tearing the other man's head from his shoulders. Eventually, Daniel let the curtains fall back into place so he could stand behind Milt's chair. "Them bodies were tacked onto the tally where those Indian attacks were concerned. Some more were found over the next few weeks, all piled up around stages that were looted or wagons containing shipments that had turned up missing."

"The Indians robbed those folks and killed them?" Slocum asked.

When Milt nodded, the gesture looked as if an invisible hand was waggling his head around. "You got that right. What's so hard to believe?"

"It isn't," Slocum said.

"I've seen plenty of Indian attacks," Daniel said. "So have the other scouts I rode with. Some of those men could track down anything on two legs through a trail that had been washed away by a flood, and even they weren't convinced we should have gone to Misty Creek after no Pawnee."

"Incompetence ain't my concern," Milt said.

Slocum kicked the gunman's chair and snapped, "Shut up!" To Daniel, he said, "But you went to Misty Creek anyway. To have a word with the Pawnee?"

Daniel nodded. "These Pawnee we spoke to weren't known for doing much of anything but farming and dancing. They traded with the local towns and didn't stir up a ruckus if they were asked to leave. Major Dwight Garrison led my unit to one of them villages along Misty Creek based on an eyewitness account that said those Injuns were the ones that stopped a group of three wagons headed into the Dakotas and sent eleven souls to meet their Maker." Rage boiled to Daniel's surface as he lashed out with one boot to kick Milt's leg hard enough to scoot the chair a few inches across the floor. "This one right here was the witness."

Gritting his teeth at the knock his leg had taken, Milt said, "Just performing my civic duty."

"Don't you know when to keep quiet?" Slocum asked.

Milt gnawed on the inside of his mouth while staring at the floor between his boots.

Looking over to Daniel, Slocum asked, "So what did your witness lead you into? An ambush?"

"More like a slaughterhouse," the scout replied. "That village didn't know what was coming or why we were there. The men that didn't ride out to greet us peacefully were too old to do much more than watch. This son of a bitch in front of me right now pointed a finger at one of the Pawnee hunters, and Major Garrison gave the order to open fire."

"Jesus."

As Daniel continued to speak, his eyes glazed over with the memories his words invoked. "That village was wiped out in a matter of minutes. Me and two other men I've known for years barely had a chance to ask what the hell was happening before we were ordered to help set the place to the torch. There wasn't even enough time to question that order. Pretty soon, I was damn near choking on the smell of all that blood."

Knowing what type of man Milt was, Slocum watched him carefully until a hint of a smirk appeared on the gunman's face. A simple shake of his head was all Slocum needed to do to warn the gunman not to press Daniel any further.

"In the week that followed . . . perhaps it was ten days . . . two more villages were hit," Daniel explained. "Each one was burnt down the same as the first. Seemed worse, though, because I knew what was coming."

"God damn," Slocum whispered. "Now I recall reading something about that in a newspaper. The Misty Creek Massacre, it was called."

Daniel nodded. "Major Garrison kept trying to get me to join in on the killing. Most of the rest of the unit was plenty happy to do it themselves. Some of those men had lost friends or loved ones to Indian attacks throughout the years. Some didn't think to disobey their orders. Others were just plain bloodthirsty. The major didn't like it that me and Cullen wouldn't take part. After the third village, talk began circulating about us being cowards or traitors."

"You don't think those Pawnee were responsible for those attacks," Slocum pointed out.

"I couldn't say that for certain," Daniel said. "But even if they were, that don't justify what happened to those three villages. I don't rightly know how many Indians were killed when those places were put to the torch. Major Garrison was brought up on charges, but they were dropped on account of some bureaucratic nonsense. The major even admitted there may have been a mistake, but he blamed it on bad information given to his men by the eyewitness." Punctuating his next words by kicking Milt's chair, Daniel added, "*This* eyewitness."

"I saw what I saw," Milt grunted.

"If the testimony and evidence held up," Slocum said reluctantly, "there's not a lot for you to do about it. I'm not going to be a party to a lynching."

"If that's what I wanted, I could have gunned him down in the street," Daniel said. "There was no evidence to back the story about the Pawnee being behind the attack. Not after me and a few other men with experience in Indian attacks took a closer look. And as for the testimony, it came from a handful of men that were all as disreputable as this idiot right here. By the looks of it, there was something else behind those villages being burnt to the ground than what we previously thought."

"And the case still held up?"

"There wasn't anyone left to prosecute. Major Garrison turned his back long enough for a gang of three-legged tortoises to get away. When he was asked to pick up the hunt for the fraudulent witnesses and commit troops to tracking them down along with anyone else who might have steered things in the wrong direction where Misty Creek was concerned, he insisted it was a waste of precious manpower and resources. A few more attacks happened in scattered parts of Nebraska and Kansas, so he sank his teeth into those.

And since nobody was left alive to speak up for them Pawnee, the Army was happy to let the ugly matter fade away."

"So that's it?" Slocum asked.

For the first time since Daniel had introduced himself to Slocum, the scout showed him a genuine smile. "Not hardly. There's still a case open. Remember that other scout that joined me in thinking something was wrong with all of this slaughter and pillaging?"

"Yeah."

"He tracked down the other two murderous pieces of shit that swore to stand by anything Major Garrison said. They're being held in a jail in a town called Culbertson a two-day ride from here. I intend on bringing this one back there to answer for what he did."

"Isn't it this Major Garrison who needs to answer for his crimes?" Slocum asked.

Daniel shifted his fiery glare to Milt. "He will. Those villages weren't burnt just to smoke out a gang of killers, so that means there's something else going on. I'd stake my life on the fact that this one here and those other outlaws locked up in Culbertson have something to do with it. Once these men are brought to justice and the Misty Creek affair is put under closer scrutiny, Garrison will be next in line for a fall."

"Ain't nobody gonna press no charges because there ain't no real charges to be pressed," Milt spat. "And even if there was, nobody cares enough to pursue 'em."

"Just because nobody wants to pursue it don't mean the case was closed," Daniel pointed out.

"We'll see who wants to pursue it once Major Garrison isn't around to watch over you."

Milt looked up at Daniel and showed him a crooked, shit-eating grin. "Word's probably already gotten back to the major about what you and that other renegade soldier has done. All he's gotta do is have you recalled. Once he tugs on your leash, you'll go scurrying away with yer tail between yer legs."

"That won't happen."

"You're still a solider. To men like me, that's in the same yard as a law dog. Long as I mind my step around you, there ain't a thing you can do. If you was a true renegade, you would'a done more than tie me to a chair and kick it around."

Slocum stepped into Milt's view like a bank of storm clouds blotting out the sun. "I'm not a soldier or a law dog," he said. "All you have to do is threaten my life and I can gun you down in self-defense. That is, if anyone's around to notice you've been shot. Plenty of dead bodies turn up in Dodge City without causing a fuss and yours wouldn't be missed. Outside of town limits, you won't be nothing but food for whatever wild animals happen to dig you up from your shallow grave."

That closed Milt's mouth for good, so Slocum looked over to Daniel and asked, "When do we leave?"

8

The rest of the night was spent with Slocum and Daniel sleeping in shifts while the other watched Milt. It was around three in the morning when Slocum swung his legs over the side of the bed to take his turn at watch duty. "Has he still been quiet or did I sleep through something exciting?" he asked.

"Everything's still quiet," Daniel replied.

Ever since Milt had dozed off in the chair with his head lolling forward, the only noise in the room was his snoring.

"What did you do with Fitz anyway?" Slocum asked.

Daniel peeked through the window and then walked over to the door so he could listen for noises in the hallway. "We tussled for a bit before I knocked him out. Damn near busted a dresser using the side of his head. He could still be sleeping it off. Didn't you say Milt was working with more than just that one fella?"

"Cameron is just some local gambler," Slocum said while standing up and stretching his back. "He didn't strike me as the sort who would stick his neck out to rescue anyone. More than likely, he'll just hire new help tomorrow."

"Well, keep alert anyhow," Daniel said while setting himself down onto the side of the bed that Slocum had just vacated. "We're leaving first thing in the morning."

"Sounds good to me."

For the rest of the night, Slocum sat in a chair with his arms folded and his senses sharp. The only sounds he heard within the Lady Gay were those that were to be expected inside any saloon. As daylight approached, folks found their way upstairs and Slocum was chomping at the bit to get Milt prepared for the journey. Daniel awoke on his own and immediately set to work.

Their prisoner didn't put up any more fuss than a petulant child. Mostly, there was a lot of squirming, spitting, and name-calling, but it wasn't long before Milt's hands were tied securely behind his back and he was being shoved down the rear stairs. Daniel had a horse being kept near the saloon, and when he was getting Milt loaded onto it, Slocum asked, "You got any money?"

"What do you need money for?" Daniel replied.

"I need a horse and can't think of anyone who's giving them away."

"Can't you rent one?"

"I need money for that, too."

"I've got some for expenses, but not much."

As Daniel dug through his pockets, Slocum looked at Milt. "Did you ever search him?"

"For weapons."

Approaching the prisoner, Slocum reached for the pockets of Milt's jacket, which immediately got Milt squirming again.

"Now you wanna rob *me?*" Milt wailed.

"Oh, stop your bellyaching," Slocum said as he riffled through Milt's jacket, shirt, and pants pockets. It didn't take long before he uncovered a few familiar items as well as a small bundle of cash.

"That's mine, you son of a bitch!" Milt groused. "Even if I was tossed into jail, my things would be kept for me."

Holding up the cash so Milt could see it before he closed a fist around it and pocketed it for himself, Slocum replied, "I'm not the law, remember? Besides, this right here," he added while showing him the familiar item, "is my watch."

Milt actually looked at the pocket watch as if he thought there was a chance that Slocum was mistaken. "Guess that's yours to take."

"What about my gun?"

"What gun?"

Slocum drew the .38 he'd taken from Milt's holster earlier and stuck its barrel against the other man's face. "It's kind of like this one, only it won't be shoved down your throat in about ten seconds."

"Cameron's got it," Milt told him.

"Why does he want it?"

"Because it belonged to you. Folks've heard your name and they'll know what it took to get your gun out of your hands."

"They'll also know I was one of the men to drag you kicking and screaming out of that alley last night and carry you out of Dodge like a prized calf strung to the back of a horse. I'm about to go rent a horse and I imagine folks will know where I got that money, too."

"That's a lot of talking."

"There'll be more than that when I come back for your friend Fitz. Was Milt carrying a gun when you found him, Daniel?" The scout stepped over to hand Slocum the .44 he'd taken from Milt the night before. Smirking, Slocum slipped the .44 into his holster and tucked the .38 under his gun belt. "Seeing as how I've now got two of your guns to replace the one I picked up a few days before I got to Dodge City, I'd say I came out ahead in this deal."

"You got enough there to rent your horse?" Daniel asked.

"Should be. Can you handle taking Milt out of town?"

Daniel nodded. "We'll be heading northwest at a decent

pace, so do your best to catch up. If it takes longer than you thought, just look for the campfire."

"I will." With that, Slocum headed toward the Lucky Days Stable by way of Front Street. He wasn't worried about losing track of Daniel and his prisoner. If the Army man wanted to shake Slocum loose before the job was done, that was his prerogative. Slocum was more concerned about crossing paths with Cameron or Fitz while strolling through town. After what had happened, it was just as likely either of the two men would take a shot at him as they would run and hide before being seen. Now that he had Milt's .44 tucked into his holster and the .38 stashed at the small of his back, Slocum wasn't worried about being able to defend himself. In fact, he thought with a self-satisfied grin, the .44 looked to be in better working condition than the pistol he'd carried into town.

Upon reaching the Lucky Days, he found Anne in the same spot she always was: tending to one of the horses inside her barn. "How much to rent that dun?" he asked.

"More than you've got," she replied. "Even if you take away what you earned already." Stopping what she was doing so she could look around at the noticeably cleaner stalls, she added, "Or maybe not. How long do you need her?"

"A few days. I'm going to Culbertson. Ever heard of it?"

"If you're staying there for more than a night or two, you'll probably need the weekly rate for the round trip. You are coming back, right?"

"That's the plan."

Shrugging once, Anne got back to her work and said, "That's good enough for me."

"It is?"

"Why? Is there a reason it shouldn't be?"

"No," Slocum told her. "You just never struck me as the sort of woman who was easy to take someone at their word."

"I'm not. That is, until someone has proven worthy of a bit of trust."

"And you think I have?"

"Yep. You're still paying for the horse. I'll need a little more than what I owe you to cover the entire weekly rate."

Slocum held up a portion of the wad he'd taken from Milt. "This be enough?"

Her eyes widened and she approached the money. "Did you rob a bank?"

"No. I robbed the asshole who knocked me in the head and took everything I was carrying."

"Oh." She took some bills and tucked them into one of her dress pockets. "So I take it you no longer need the job here."

"We'll see about that when I get back."

Slocum led the dun away from the stable and to the Dodge House. He used up most of Milt's money to square up his bill and buy a few supplies for the upcoming ride. Once his saddle and bags were buckled into place, he tipped his hat to Estrella and rode his rented dun out of town.

A few miles outside Dodge, Slocum caught up to Daniel. The winds whipped across the flat terrain, causing the tall grass to sway and shift entire fields from green to a brownish yellow as all of the blades were bent one way or another. The scout's prisoner sat in the saddle behind Daniel and seemed content to remain that way. Although he wasn't able to turn completely around to get a look at him, Daniel acknowledged Slocum with a friendly wave. "That was quick," he said.

Slocum rode alongside the other man's horse and said, "Picked up some supplies as well. Looks like you two are becoming friendly."

Daniel chuckled at that. "I told him he could either go civilly or sideways like a sack of potatoes."

"And he chose civil? Surprising."

"Well, he chose it after I introduced him to a few creative knots I was shown by a former U.S. marshal."

Now that he was closer and had had a few moments to examine Daniel's horse, Slocum could see the rope that crossed behind Milt's back to connect his wrists to the saddle in a few different spots. Having known a few U.S. marshals in his time, Slocum said, "Now that makes a lot more sense. You're smart to stay still, Milt. You fall from there and you'll probably break your arms while being dragged behind the horse."

Milt grunted something unintelligible, so Daniel said, "He learned that the hard way before we left Dodge City. Tried to roll off, but hung over the side and got both legs smashed against a water trough. If we were going any faster, he wouldn't be much more useful than that sack of spuds I mentioned earlier."

Since Milt wasn't about to join in on that conversation, he remained still and did his best to keep his balance as Daniel touched his heels to the sides of his horse. That kept the prisoner occupied for most of the day as the two hoses rode along a trail that cut through Kansas like a crooked scar.

They reined their horses to a stop at a watering hole when the sun had dipped partway below the western horizon. There was time to get a bit more riding done, but neither Slocum nor Daniel was certain if they would find a better spot to make camp. Since they figured on getting into Culbertson later the next day no matter what, it made sense to water the horses and get some rest to make up for the spotty patches of sleep they'd had the night before.

Milt was dragged off the horse's back and tied to a stump without it being necessary for the ropes to be removed from his hands. "What about givin' me a damn moment to stretch?" he groused. "Ain't I even allowed to relieve myself?"

"Go right ahead," Daniel replied. "It won't make a difference with how you already smell."

"Nice for someone else to be rancid for a change," Slocum mused.

"I'm serious," Milt said. "Tie me up however you want, but just let me squat behind some damn bushes!"

"I can arrange it," Slocum said. "You've had him connected to you all day."

After helping untie Milt from the saddle and fashioning something close to the leash he'd used in town, Daniel tipped his hat and walked in the opposite direction. "Don't mind if I do. Collecting firewood beats the living hell out of being downwind of that one."

Slocum drew the .44 and pointed it at Milt's back. "Try anything funny and I'll put one through your leg."

"Yeah, whatever," Milt grunted as he staggered behind a bush and shimmied his pants down using his thumbs along the back of his waistband. It was an awkward process, but neither man wanted it to become a joint effort. When he was done, Milt hiked up his pants, stood straight up, and started running away.

Before he tugged on the rope to take up the slack, Slocum discovered a cracked rock where Milt had anchored the rope. Some of the rope was frayed, which showed what he'd been doing while squatting and shuffling and grunting to make a bunch of noise when he should have been emptying his bowels. The rope was too strong to be cut in a short amount of time, but if Slocum had pulled it taut while Milt had taken off running at top speed, the rock may have cut deeply enough for the rope to snap.

Slocum needed only a second or two to digest this. After that, he watched as Milt ran all the way to the end of his restraint. Without Slocum adding his muscle to the task, the rock held it fast once Milt had gone as far as he could go. The prisoner's arms snapped back against his shoulder joints, creating a pain that elicited a high-pitched yelp. His progress was stopped so suddenly that Milt's feet continued to flounder and the lower portion of his body was taken out from beneath him. It was truly a sight to behold.

Even though he tightened his grip on the rope in expectation of having to reel Milt back in, Slocum mostly just got to watch as Milt hit the ground on his back in a flailing mess of churning legs. After unwinding the rope from the rock, he walked over to Milt and said, "That was a fast bit of work. Hope you also got a chance to have your squat." Before Milt could say anything in response, Slocum swung the .44 so the side of the pistol connected with the other man's temple. Milt hit the dirt in one of the most satisfying sounds Slocum could imagine.

"Damn," Daniel said as he piled some sticks to make a campfire. "I've been wanting to do that all day."

"Why didn't you?"

"Because riding would have been that much harder with him waking up and kicking all them times."

"We could always put him down so he won't kick anymore," Slocum offered.

Daniel gazed up at the darkening sky as if he was contemplating something truly inspirational. Then, he started piling the sticks he'd collected and said, "Nah. We already came this far. Might as well see it through."

Slocum rolled Milt onto his back so he could drag him closer to the camp and then hog-tie him with the rope that was already secured around his wrists. By the time Milt was wrapped up and propped in a more or less upright stance, the campfire was crackling.

"So why are you doing this?" Daniel asked.

"You're only asking me this now?"

"I figured you might have changed your mind before meeting up with us or parted ways somewhere before getting this far. It's not like you have much stake in this mess. I know Milt robbed you and all, but you could have just reclaimed your belongings and been on your way."

"That would have been the sensible thing to do," Slocum replied. "But I rarely take that road."

Daniel stretched out so his legs were crossed in front of him, and he clasped his hands behind his head. Reclining as if he were on a cushion, he gazed up at a sky that was shifting from deep purple to a dark royal blue. A few stars could be seen and the moon hung among them in all its glory. "Even when I hear myself spell out what I'm doing wrapped up in this, it sometimes don't seem enough for me to throw away my career."

"Is that what you're doing?"

Daniel let out a heavy sigh. "More than likely. The best way for this to end is for everyone involved to be locked up with no loose ends on the outside to take any orders from the men that were jailed. I've been in a uniform for too long to think a man like Major Garrison didn't get to where he is without making any friends."

"Could be those friends will cut him loose once everything comes out in the open."

"And that would be fine by me."

Slocum went over to his horse so he could rummage through his saddlebags to retrieve a can of beans and some coffee. "You don't think that's how this will turn out, though, do you?"

"I've got my hopes, but I ain't about to hold my breath. A friend of mine once called that cautious optimism."

"I call it not being a damn fool."

Both men laughed, but were silenced when Milt began to stir. The prisoner grunted and flopped over like a pig that was too fat to be supported by its own legs, which made Slocum and Daniel laugh even harder. From then on, Slocum went through the paces of preparing their simple dinner.

"You still didn't answer my question," Daniel pointed out. "Why are you going through all of this trouble?"

"Because I believe your story about what happened at Misty Creek."

"Too many people believe me, but not a lot of them are willing to do anything about it."

"I don't like it when men think they can get away with murdering innocents for any reason. And when an opportunity presents itself for me to put some of those men in their place, you'd be amazed at what I'm willing to do."

Daniel studied him for a few more seconds before shifting his focus back to the sky. "I think we'll get along just fine."

9

Milt woke up sometime after supper had been eaten and cleared away. If only to keep the prisoner from griping all night long, Slocum prepared a plate of beans and poured some coffee into a cup. Since Milt needed his hands free to eat, Daniel watched him over the barrel of a shotgun that he carried in the boot of his saddle. Slocum had to give the gunman credit. If he were in Milt's shoes, he'd have a much tougher time getting his food down while staring down that barrel. Milt, on the other hand, asked for seconds.

"You're lucky you got firsts," Slocum said to the request. "Now hold your hands behind your back so I can tie you up again."

"At least let me keep them in front."

"It doesn't make a difference when you're laying down. Just shut up and get some sleep."

"What if I ain't tired?"

"I said you'd be down," Slocum told him. "I can accomplish that by asking you or putting you down like I did when you tried scampering off like a damn fool. Which would you prefer?"

Milt preferred to grumble under his breath as his hands were tied securely behind his back. There was a minimum of conversation after that. Milt kicked and fretted before finding a comfortable spot. Slocum and Daniel had already developed an effective system of guard duty, so they traded off sleeping while the other watched the camp and the prisoner.

Morning announced itself with the sun's rays jabbing at Slocum's eyelids. He awoke to find Daniel sloshing the remaining coffee in the pot before pouring some into a cup. Slocum walked over to Milt and nudged him with his toe. When the prisoner didn't move, he gave him a solid kick with the side of his foot.

Milt sprang into motion with an attempt to trip Slocum with a powerful kick across his ankles. Slocum only needed to hop back a step while drawing the .44. "Appreciate that, Milt," he said. "Always good to get the blood flowing so early in the morning."

"And just for that," Daniel added, "here's your coffee." He splashed the brew onto the prisoner's face and then refilled the cup so he could hand it over to Slocum.

"It's cold!" Milt snapped.

"Good. Should I serve breakfast the same way?"

"No," Milt replied in a surprisingly meek tone.

Still carrying the .44 in one hand, Slocum walked around to stand behind Milt while drawing his knife with the other. "You ready?"

After scooping some leftover beans onto a plate and setting it down, Daniel picked up his shotgun and took a few steps back. He nodded, which prompted Slocum to cut the rope with a single downward slash from the blade. Milt rubbed his wrists as if they'd been sheared of flesh and then grabbed the plate so he could use his fingers to scoop the beans into his mouth.

Breakfast was one of the biggest reasons Slocum liked

staying in town. Although there was something to be said about a skillet of hot bacon or flapjacks cooked on an open fire, days that got started with cold beans and gritty coffee from the night before weren't exactly memorable. There were other pros and cons in the debate between hotel and camp, but that one stuck out to Slocum the most as he picked cold coffee grounds from between his teeth. He was all too glad to toss the rest of the beans into the grass before breaking camp and saddling the horses while Daniel prepared Milt with his special knotting technique.

"There's less rope than last time on account of him cutting it," Milt griped.

"Don't worry," Daniel said. "Just cinches you in tighter."

"Too tight! I'm bent over like a damned hunchback!"

"And you'd best keep still because if you fall from the saddle in this state, you'll wind up a cripple."

That kept Milt quiet for the duration of the day's ride.

One of the best things about Kansas being so flat was that a horse could cover a whole lot of distance in a short amount of time. Slocum let his rented dun stretch her legs at a full gallop, and the only reason he needed to slow down was to periodically let Daniel and his reluctant passenger catch up. Milt hung on for dear life, gritting his teeth and wincing as every third step made him slip one way or another. From what he'd seen of the series of knots Daniel had tied, Slocum guessed there weren't too many ways for the bound man to fall. Even so, a little bit of panic on Milt's part made for a much smoother journey.

By early evening, the silhouette of Culbertson broke the skyline into a short series of squat buildings and a row of tall poles that extended for a quarter of a mile alongside the trail to the east and west. Owing to the flat landscape, catching sight of the town didn't mean they were almost there. It was another hour or so before they were close enough for Slocum to tell there weren't any wires hanging from the tops of those poles. A few minutes after that, they were close enough to smell civilization.

"Wherever that beef is bein' cooked, take me to it!" Milt demanded. "I don't care if you toss me into that place just the way I am, I gotta get some real food in my belly."

"That doesn't sound half bad," Slocum said. "Up for a steak, Daniel?"

Although he drew in the fragrant scent longingly, Daniel shook his head and kept his horse pointed down the trail that had since become Main Street and ran from one end of town to the other. "I didn't bring this asshole along to feed him. He can get something to eat once he's locked up."

"Aw, for Christ's sake," Milt whined. "I came along this far without much of a fuss. The least you could do is buy me a decent meal with the money Slocum picked from my pockets!"

"First of all," Slocum said, "you've tried to escape more than once, which counts as quite a lot of fuss. Second, most of that money in your pockets was mine in the first place, and third, the least I could do is—"

"Yeah, yeah," Milt groaned. "You could shoot me in the head, bury me somewhere, and let the dogs dig me up. That one's wearing thin."

"Which doesn't make it any less true."

"Fine, then. If you ain't gonna feed me, then get me locked away so I don't have to listen to any more of the shit that keeps spilling from your mouths."

The source of the delectable scents that had caught their attention seemed to be a small place called Bullseye Saloon and Steaks. Slocum nodded toward it and asked, "Meet you inside when you're through?"

"Sounds good."

"Jesus," Milt groaned. "Get me behind bars before you two start swappin' spit."

Daniel was all too happy to oblige and he snapped his reins to keep riding farther into town while Slocum tied his horse to a post near a water trough. The dun lapped grate-fully as Slocum stepped into the Bullseye. Almost imme-diately, he was struck by a wave of smoky scents mixed liberally with something else that made it even better. A young woman with straight red hair approached him and smiled while asking, "What can I do for you?"

"You can tell me that's cornbread I'm smelling."

"Sure is. A fresh batch just came from the oven."

"Then you just made my day."

"Like a seat at a table?" she asked.

"And a feed bag. Speaking of which, where might I be able to put my horse up for the night?"

"Depends on where you're staying," the redhead told him as she scooped up some utensils and led Slocum to a table by the window. "If you intend on getting a room at the Whis-pering Hill, they'll take good care of your horse. There's a livery down on Third that charges a fair price, but if you're just passing through for something to eat, I can have some-one fetch some oats for you."

"It's been a long day, so see to them oats. Just tack it on to my bill."

Her smile was wide, and her lips were a dark shade of red. Both of those things competed for Slocum's attention as she set a menu down onto the table and started to walk away.

"Mind if I take that seat right over there?" he asked while pointing to a smaller table situated against the back wall.

She looked at it, shrugged, and then gathered up all the things she'd set down. "Most folks prefer a view."

"I just came off of a two-day ride. I've had all the view I can stomach."

"Fair enough. Our special is pork chops and creamed corn."

"Does that come with cornbread?" Slocum asked.

"If you like."

"I like. Bring me that and some water."

"And I like a man who knows what he wants," she said while cradling the menu in one arm and walking away amid the bustle of swaying hips and swirling skirts.

So far, Slocum was glad to be in Culbertson.

It was a bit past supper time, which meant the Bullseye was down to its customers who preferred to be served from a bottle. A short bar ran along the back of the place, and a set of tall, narrow doors led into the kitchen. A few lonely souls stood at the bar nursing their drinks, and there seemed to be a poker game being played in one of the rear corners of the room. Since that was about all of the life in there besides Slocum and the employees, he guessed there must have been a rowdier saloon somewhere else in town. The pork chop special came promptly and was devoured in short order. The plate of cornbread that had been brought to his table lasted about as long as a tall glass of water split between a dozen riders crossing the Mojave Desert. Although the redhead had checked on him a few times throughout his meal, she eventually kept her distance as though Slocum were a ravenous dog that didn't want its bone taken away before it had been stripped it of every last scrap of meat.

"Where's the law around here?" he asked when she passed nearby.

"Why?" she asked. "Do you have a complaint?"

"No, a friend of mine was supposed to be meeting me here after paying a visit to your town's law."

Relieved that she or her workplace wasn't in the crosshairs, she told him, "That'd be Sheriff Teaghan. His office is at the corner of Main and Virginia."

Slocum approached the window and looked outside. Instinct more than anything else caused him to peek through the edge of the curtains without placing too much of his body in sight of anyone keeping watch on that pane of glass. "Which direction is Virginia?" he asked.

"It's one street down that way," she replied while pointing toward the west end of town. "You should be able to see it from here. It's the one with all the horses tied out front."

"Got it," Slocum said, having already spotted Daniel's horse. He watched for a few more seconds before the redhead tentatively approached him.

"Are you expecting trouble?" she asked.

"No, my friend is just late." As a way to steer her away from what may or may not be a problem, Slocum added, "How about you round up another basket of the cornbread for when he arrives?"

"You already ate your share," said another woman from the back of the saloon. She wore a rumpled apron that covered her from a few inches below her neck to a few inches above her feet and was spattered with enough flour, grease, and other stains to mark her as the Bullseye's cook. Curly blond hair was held back in a tail, but many strands had come loose to hang against her cheeks or bounce along her forehead. Judging by the expression on her softly rounded face, she wasn't as happy to cook more cornbread as Slocum was to eat it.

"I'll pay my bill if that's what you're worried about," Slocum said. "This is for a friend of mine."

"The bill's not my concern. It's his," the blonde said while waving a hand toward the bar.

A tall scarecrow of a man behind the bar waved both hands in the air above his balding head and hollered, "For Pete's sake, let the man alone, Bethany!"

"Pete's sake and mine," Slocum chided.

Although the redhead giggled under her breath, Bethany wasn't so easily appeased. "Dinner's over, mister," she said. "Either take what we got left or go somewhere else. If you don't like it, you should've come at a more reasonable hour."

"Bethany!" the bartender barked.

"Fine," she said while turning back toward the kitchen. "I suppose nobody else gets to carry on with their lives if some cowboy rides in and has to have a home-cooked meal."

"If this food wasn't the best I'd tasted in three months, I'd tell you to stick it all where the sun don't shine," Slocum said. "But since it is, I'd be grateful for you to fix another plate of it for my friend."

At first, Bethany was put off by the backhanded compliment. Once it settled in, however, a flicker of a smile drifted across her face. She didn't have any more cross words for him while she quickly got to work on another daily special. When she emerged from the kitchen again, she carried a dinner plate covered by a tin lid and ready to go. "One more serving of pork chops," she announced while approaching Slocum.

He stood by the window, having spent his time watching the street in front of the sheriff's office while the food had been prepared. Turning toward the clatter of the plate being set down onto the closest table, he drew a breath to speak but didn't need to ask his next question.

"And," Bethany cut in, "here's your cornbread."

Slocum was still holding the curtain as he looked toward the table that had been the redhead's first choice when seating him. On top of the covered plate was a bundle wrapped in napkins held in place with a piece of string. "Much obliged," he said.

"Just don't think you'll get special treatment again," Bethany said as she waggled a finger at him. "You've been warned. Once my kitchen is closed, it's—"

A gunshot blasted from the street to shatter the glass.

The bullet that had been fired chipped a jagged hole through the pane and passed so close between Slocum and Bethany that he could hear it hiss by as it entered the saloon, shattered a glass on one table, and became lodged in a wall. Slocum dropped the food he'd been holding and threw himself at Bethany since she was the only other one standing with him at the window.

The redhead screamed and covered her head with her hands. Customers at the bar hunkered down as if to protect their drinks as the men playing cards in the back of the room dove for the floor. Slocum saw this in bits and pieces as he brought Bethany down. When he hit the floor on his shoulder, the closest thing to his face was the covered plate, which had somehow survived the fall. He twisted around to find Bethany lying nearby after having dropped and rolled a bit to one side.

"You all right?" he asked.

"My arm hurts. I think I landed on it."

"No! Are you hit?"

She wriggled, but didn't act like someone who'd taken a bullet. "No," she said to confirm Slocum's suspicions. "I don't think so."

"Then—"

More shots blasted through the window, punching holes through it while sending a rain of chipped glass down onto Slocum's head, back, and shoulders.

At the back of the room, the balding barkeep stuck his head up like a prairie dog that had chosen the worst possible time to emerge from its hole. "Son of a bitch!" he shouted. "Do you know how expensive that window was?"

"Wanna tell it to the man outside or get your head back down?" Slocum replied.

Even though the barkeep seemed to take a moment to ponder which choice he preferred, he rushed to a conclusion when another barrage of gunshots blasted through the saloon.

"Stay here," Slocum said to Bethany.

"Where else would I go? Wait a second!" she cried. "You should stay here, too!"

But Slocum wasn't listening. He'd already kicked open the door and charged into the fray.

10

Slocum was no stranger to carrying a pistol in each hand, and he sure as hell knew better than to discharge both weapons at the same time. On special occasions, however, unleashing a torrent of noise and smoke was preferable to taking the time to place his rounds correctly. Since all he wanted was to draw fire away from the front of the Bullseye, he gripped the .38 and .44 he'd taken from Milt and announced his presence with an eruption of blazing fury.

There were two men standing in the street. One carried a rifle and the other had a smoking pistol, which they'd used to shatter the expensive front window. A spattering of rain had started to fall, which turned the street into a shallow river of mud. Slocum's first shot surprised them and the ones that followed had come so quickly that both men could only scatter for cover before one of the wild rounds could find its mark. One dove behind a water trough and the other made it to one of the thick posts that formed a dotted line through the middle of town.

"Only two of you?" Slocum yelled after he'd emptied three rounds from each pistol. "Usually when a bunch of cowards fire into a room full of unarmed people, there's at least three or four in the pack."

Having placed his back to a pole, the man with the rifle swung around to fire at Slocum. That prompted the man behind the trough to ditch his pistol in favor of a shotgun that he'd either tossed ahead of him or kept stashed nearby. However he'd carried it, the double barrels made a hell of a noise when they belched their smoky payload.

Slocum ducked back into the saloon, but just far enough to find some cover in the doorway. The rifle round knocked into the wall a foot or two away from him, but the scatter-gun's pellets came from too far away to do more than smack against the front of the place like hard rain. As soon as Slocum started to poke his nose out to return fire, another shot was fired from across the street that hadn't been sent by either of the two men he'd spotted.

"There you are!" Slocum hollered.

Whoever the third man was, he remained hidden as he shouted, "You're not welcome here! Get on your horse and leave town now or there'll be hell to pay."

"Do you speak for the town's welcoming committee?"

That joke was met with another volley of gunfire, some of which found its way through the broken window of the Bullseye. Since his intention had been to keep anyone inside from getting killed, Slocum grit his teeth, tightened his grip on both pistols, and ran for the pole that was closest to him. One or two of the shots got a bit too close for his comfort, but the men outside were more concerned with making noise than spilling blood. As soon as they ran dry, Slocum stepped out and fired the proper way.

Rather than send as much lead as possible toward the attackers, he sighted along the top of the .44 and fired at the man who'd sought shelter behind the next pole down the street. The wooden column was thick enough to keep the head-level shot from penetrating all the way through, so Slocum lowered his aim to the edge of the pole where the man wasn't able to benefit from the most solid portion of his cover. The side of the pole splintered into bits as Slocum's round punched through it as well as the meaty portion of the man's thigh. The gunman swore to high heaven and lost interest in the fight.

Then, Slocum fired at the water trough, but was thrown off his aim when the man behind it, who'd switched away from his shotgun to a pistol, fired at him. Since the .44 was empty, Slocum holstered it and made a border shift by tossing the .38 from his left hand to his right. As soon as his finger touched the trigger, he fired his rounds in quick succession. Each hit the trough to form a series of holes that started at the upper edge of the large wooden container and ended with a hole that punched through the trough as well as the man lying behind it.

Although seeing the man roll away from the trough while grabbing his upper arm was a welcome sight, Slocum knew there was still at least one more gunman to deal with and he hadn't been able to pin down exactly where that one was hiding.

"Your ammo is spent," the hidden man shouted. "That is, unless you're carrying a third pistol."

"Wanna gamble your life that I'm not?" Slocum asked.

"He don't need one," Daniel shouted from the street. He carried his rifle with the stock against his shoulder and ready to fire. "I've got a line on these two in front of me, and the moment you show your face, I'll have a line on you, too. Reckon that'll give you enough time to reload, John?"

"More than enough," Slocum replied as his hands went through the motions of replacing the spent rounds in the .44 with fresh ones he'd purchased in Dodge City.

After a heavy pause, the hidden shooter said, "This was just a warning. Next time you won't be allowed to walk away."

"You delivered your message and we heard it just fine," Slocum said. "Whether or not you live to see tomorrow is up to you."

Each of Slocum's senses was heightened by the blood surging through his veins and the excitement that had been packed into the last few minutes. His eyes were trained on the darkened shadows across the street in front of him, and his ears strained for any hint that another volley of gunfire might be on its way. When he saw a glint near the top of one of the buildings across from the Bullseye, he fired reflexively.

"Hold your fire!" a man shouted from Daniel's end of the street. He was several inches shorter than Daniel, but carried himself like the cock of the walk. The tin star pinned to his chest only furthered that claim.

Both of the wounded men struggled to get away, but neither could get more than a few steps before Slocum and Daniel had them covered. "Sheriff Teaghan," Daniel announced. "Best bring the rest of your men out to deal with this."

Although Teaghan had his gun drawn, he seemed just as ready to fire at Slocum or Daniel as he was to take a shot at anyone else. "You don't tell me what to do, son. I only just met you. Who the hell are you?"

Since the sheriff's eyes were pointed at him, Slocum shouted his name, followed by, "These other two shot the hell out of this saloon and could have killed any number of folks inside. For all I know, someone is hit in there."

"Then we'd best go in and have a look."

"What about that other man across the street?"

"What other man is that?"

Although he couldn't see any more now as compared to a few moments ago, Slocum's gut told him that the third shooter was gone. That didn't stop him from saying, "He's somewhere on the second floor of that building!"

Teaghan walked down the street as if he couldn't smell the burnt gunpowder still hanging in the air. Standing between Slocum and the building in question, he squinted up at the second floor and said, "Don't look like anyone's there now."

"That's because he got away!"

"From where I stand, you men need to worry more about explaining yourselves and less about the one that got away." When Daniel stepped onto the boardwalk and headed toward the Bullseye, Teaghan asked, "Where the hell are you going?"

"I had a long ride, Sheriff. I planned on getting something to eat."

"What about this mess?"

"You need me to explain myself for the couple of seconds I wasn't with you helping to toss that piece of shit I dragged all the way from Dodge City behind bars? Here's my explanation. I heard the same gunshots you did, came out to see what was happening, and found my partner in the middle of a shooting gallery. You showed up and . . . that's about it."

Teaghan sputtered as Daniel continued to step past Slocum and into the saloon, but wasn't about to try and impede his progress. Instead, he shifted his ire toward the next available target. "What about you?"

"My story's pretty much the same except I was inside minding my own business when the shooting started. I came out to investigate and found those two standing out here, pretty as you please." Slocum actually got his hopes up when the lawman glanced over to the two shooters as if he'd only just realized they were there.

"Wes?" Teaghan asked. "Benjamin? Explain yourselves."

"We heard someone was coming to bust out them killers you got in the jail, Sheriff," the man behind the water trough said as he struggled to get to his feet while grasping the bloody wound in his upper arm.

"What about you, Ben?"

"I heard the same thing."

"Well, that one there brought one of those killers in from

Dodge," the sheriff explained while waving toward the door that Daniel had just used. "Tossed him into a cell like the prettiest Christmas present I ever saw. Said he was riding with another man by the name of John Slocum. That seems to be him, which means we got ourselves a real bad case of crossed lines of communication."

Slocum stood his ground, waiting for the next round of conflicting stories. At the very least, he expected one of the shooters to get anxious on account of the pain from their wounds or the pressure of being under so much scrutiny. Rather than make a poorly chosen move, both of the wounded men lowered their heads and weapons.

"Yeah," Wes said. "Looks like it was a bad mistake."

"You men are bleeding," Teaghan said. "Best go see Don Marsh. Donnie's a retired Army medic, Mr. Slocum. Ain't exactly a doctor by the strictest sense of the word, but he's trained well enough to patch up a few flesh wounds. You need patching?"

"No, I don't need patching," Slocum fired back. "And I don't need any more of this nonsense about crossed communications. Those two opened fire on a restaurant full of people!"

"We saw you in the window," Benjamin grunted while being helped to his feet by the other shooter. "You were armed and we thought you were a killer. We ain't gunmen, so we thought to frighten you out of town."

"Thought you caught sight of us through the window and reached for your pistol," Wes continued. "The rest was poor judgment. We'll scrape together enough to cover the damages."

"There you go," the lawman shouted into the Bullseye. "The damages to the window will be covered."

"It best be a prompt payment," the skinny barkeep shouted back from just inside the place. "It ain't like I can conduct business with the wind and dust blowing through."

"Get your window replaced as soon as you can and I'll

see to it you're reimbursed," Teaghan said. "If you have trouble putting the money together, let me know and I'll have a word with whoever you deal with in that regard. Will you be going to Bob Nillewaithe?"

"Probably."

Too frustrated to contain himself for another moment, Slocum exclaimed, "That's all fine and good for the window! What's going to be done about the shooting?"

Teaghan placed his hands on his hips and replied, "Since nobody was hurt, I'm certain there will be fines that need to be paid. Other than that, you'll just have to simmer down and let me do my job, Mr. . . . ."

"Slocum."

"Right. Now all of you hand over your weapons. Whoever ain't being tended for wounds will come with me. Looks like we're all in for a long night."

Slocum didn't even touch his gun until Wes and Benjamin had handed over theirs. Even then, he was reluctant to do so until he got a nod from Daniel. He may not have known much about the former Army scout, but Daniel had done right by him so far. He took some comfort knowing a knife was still secreted in his boot.

11

The retired medic paid a visit to the sheriff's office to patch up Wes and Benjamin, who stuck to their story about thinking they were doing the town a favor by scaring away a potential threat. Both shooters also denied the idea that there was a third man across the street taking potshots at Slocum with a rifle. Even more maddening than the lies themselves was Sheriff Teaghan's willingness to eat them up like biscuits and honey.

After two hours of swapping stories inside a long building situated in front of a small jail and a short row of outhouses, Sheriff Teaghan gave one last look at the papers on which he'd been scribbling and nodded. "I guess that about sums it up."

"Does it?" Daniel asked.

"Yep. You're all free to go."

Slocum hopped up from his chair. "What did you say?"

"You heard me. Unless you change your tone, I'll think twice about letting you go."

Feeling like he was being scolded by a schoolteacher, Slocum fought back the urge to throw over the sheriff's desk and storm from the office. Instead, he gnashed his teeth together and asked, "So nobody around here cares about two men walking up and shooting out the front of a saloon?"

"Of course I give a damn about that," Teaghan said with a scowl that rivaled Slocum's. "I know these two, and if either of them try to leave town before that window is fixed, I'll personally hunt them down like dogs and string them up from the highest rafter in town. As it is, my jailhouse is stuffed full."

Having caught sight of the jailhouse on his way in to the office, Slocum wondered how more than three prisoners could be kept in there without them stepping on each other's toes. For what it was worth, at least one part of the lawman's edict was easy to swallow. "What about me?" he asked.

"Near as I can tell, you were caught in a bad spot at a bad time," the sheriff said. "On behalf of myself and the town of Culbertson, I sincerely apologize."

Before Slocum could tell the sheriff precisely where to stick that apology, Daniel asked, "We're free to come and go as we see fit?"

"Absolutely."

"And our weapons?"

"Will be returned right now." Taking the lawman's cue, a younger man with severe features stepped up to hand over Slocum's and Daniel's guns.

"What about the man I brought you?" Daniel asked. "Or the others that were brought here earlier?"

"They're still in custody as I showed you when you arrived," Teaghan replied. "And that's where they'll stay until Judge Whetuski gets in from Wichita. They'll get their trial and a noose around their necks if necessary."

"I think I'll stay in town so I can see that for myself," Daniel told him.

"Whether you stay or go, that's what's gonna happen. This is all part of my job and I know how to see it through."

"So you keep insisting," Slocum grumbled.

"Do you have a problem, mister?"

When the sheriff asked that question, his deputy stiffened as if he was preparing either to back the lawman in case of any more trouble or to get out of Teaghan's way if his mood got any worse.

Since it was clear there was nothing to be gained by doing otherwise, Slocum shook his head. "No problem here. I'll be in town, so just let me know if you need anything."

With a wide, self-satisfied smile, Teaghan proclaimed, "My deputy and I have everything well in hand, but thank you for the offer."

Slocum left the sheriff's office and walked down Main Street. Daniel emerged directly behind him and rushed for a few steps to catch up. "What do you want to do from here?" he asked.

Without breaking stride or glancing over at the other man, Slocum said, "I plan on getting a room for myself and a stall for my horse."

"No, I mean about the rest of it. Are you really staying on for a while?"

"Yes, and since you have so much more invested in this than I do, I'd suggest you do the same."

"Oh, I plan on it. In fact, the man who helped bring in some of the others filling that jail should be coming back to town shortly. His name's Cullen. You've already done so much so if you'd rather—"

Slocum stopped so quickly and spun around that Daniel almost ran into him. "We've already been through this business about me explaining my motives. Even if I'd wanted to be done with this job before, what happened in front of that saloon changed my mind right quick. I don't know about you, but I'm not so quick to forgive and forget when someone tries to blow my head off."

"I know exactly what you're saying," Daniel said.

Even though nobody was following them and neither of the lawmen had stepped out of Teaghan's office, Slocum lowered his voice as if there was still a chance of being overheard. "There was a third gunman shooting at me earlier. I heard him. I even saw a hint of him. This is too small of a town for that many killers to be rattling around without the law knowing about them."

"You think Teaghan had something to do with you being shot at?"

"I don't know if he had any direct part of it, but if he was inept enough for that sort of thing to happen within sight of his office, the law would have been cleaned out of this town long ago. I can tell you one thing for certain," Slocum added while looking in the general direction of the building across the street from the Bullseye Saloon. "That so-called lawman isn't as stupid as he looks."

A few moments passed where it seemed Slocum was going to storm away in a huff. Then, Daniel gave him a good-natured swat on the shoulder, which prompted both of them to share a tired laugh. "Do you know where you'll be staying?" Daniel asked.

"Not yet, but I'll ask over at the Bullseye. What about you?"

"Since you're staying here to keep watch on the town, I'll ride out to see if I can't catch up with Cullen. He should be on his way back here or may even be camping nearby after dropping off his prisoners. Perhaps he can help us figure out what's going on around here."

Grudgingly, Slocum admitted, "Could just be that this is a small town with a lazy sheriff guarding it. Wouldn't be the first one of those."

"Either way, this place should be just fine without me in it for a day or so. When I get back, I'll stop by that saloon with the broken window. I'm sure they'll remember you if I drop your name."

The two men shook hands and parted ways. Slocum walked down Main Street toward the Bullseye, and Daniel headed back to where his horse was tied outside the sheriff's office.

As he approached the saloon, Slocum could hear plenty of voices and activity from within the place. Some of the noise was obviously business as usual, and the rest came from those who were cleaning up or heatedly discussing the shoot-out that had occurred. When Slocum pulled open the door and stepped inside, every conversation stopped.

The first to break the silence was the balding man behind the bar. "You bring my money for that window?"

"No," Slocum replied as he walked past tables filled with people who were either drinking, playing cards, or socializing, "but it seems the broken glass didn't scare any customers away."

Most of those patrons looked at Slocum with the wide-eyed wonder someone might reserve for a circus act. Now that the smoke had cleared, they'd more than likely come by to feel like they were part of the excitement. For some, all they wanted was to be able to tell folks later on that they were sitting in a saloon where real gunmen had traded shots. After all, small towns like Culbertson might not ever get to see a genuine circus.

"Yeah," the barkeep said as he lowered his head and placed both hands flat upon his bar. "But I still need to replace that window."

"In case you've already forgotten, I'm not the one who broke it. How about a whiskey?"

The barkeep's face twisted as if it had been pruned. A series of quick, light steps moved behind the bar. "You've been griping about that damn window all night long," Bethany said as she moved to drop a hand onto the barkeep's shoulder. "Give it a rest and count your blessings that nobody was hurt during all that shooting."

"Nobody was hurt, you say?" Slocum said while focusing on the blond woman's face. "That's good to hear."

"Just a few bumps and bruises when folks dropped to the floor or tripped all over themselves to get behind something, but no more than that."

"Yeah, but—" the barkeep muttered. When Bethany raised a finger to place it against his narrow mouth, he flushed angrily.

She knew he was mad, but was more amused than threatened by it. "Nobody wants to hear more about the window. And in case you forgot, Mr. Slocum was the one who kept things from getting worse when he chased those gunmen away. For that reason, if you charge him one red cent for that whiskey, I will slap the taste out of your mouth."

One of the other men at the bar laughed heartily and bellowed, "She's got you there, Slick!"

Considering the sour turn his facial expression had taken, the barkeep liked that nickname even less than the prospect of handing out free liquor. Even so, he poured the drink without scolding the customer as the rest of the Bullseye worked itself back up to its former noisy state.

Slocum held up the drink to Bethany when she leaned forward to take the spot the balding man had vacated. "Appreciate the assistance," he told her. "After all the bullshit I've been forced to endure lately, I was about to break another window by tossing ol' Slick straight through it."

"Couldn't hurt to shake some of the rocks loose from between his ears."

"You seem awfully chipper for someone who was nearly shot," Slocum said. "In fact, you were in a fouler mood when I asked for another plate of pork chops."

"Nearly getting killed made that other nonsense seem petty. All right," she added with a smile that snuck up on Slocum almost as well as she'd snuck up on the barkeep, "it was petty no matter how you look at it. Why haven't you finished your drink?"

"Because something tells me it's the only free one I'll be getting."

"Not as long as I'm standing here."

Just to test that theory, Slocum brought the glass to his mouth and upended it. The fire water burned down his throat to warm a trail all the way down to his stomach. Within seconds after he'd set the glass down, Bethany filled it up again. By the time he tipped that drink to her by way of a silent thank-you, she'd poured one for herself.

After drinking half of her whiskey, she closed her eyes and let out a satisfied breath. "And that just made me feel even better."

Slocum chuckled and waved off the offer for her to pour another dose of whiskey for him. "I don't suppose you have rooms to rent in this place?"

"There's one, but you wouldn't want it. Mostly, it's a place to toss someone who's too drunk to walk out the door or too randy to bring a whore to a proper bed. Try the Whispering Hills further down the street. It's about halfway between here and the sheriff's office. I'm guessing you already know where the sheriff's office is."

When Slocum left the Bullseye, all he needed to do was walk his horse straight down Main Street. From what he could tell from his limited tour of Culbertson, there wasn't much else in town other than Main Street. He didn't have far to walk before spotting the Whispering Hills Hotel. It was smaller than he'd been expecting. Part of his perception may have come from the fact that he'd grown accustomed to the larger hotels in Dodge City. Another part was that Whispering Hills was just damn small.

About half the size of the Bullseye, the two-story building was clean, quiet, and smelled like freshly cleaned linens. The front desk was an old roll-top model situated just inside the front door a few paces away from a staircase. The woman who sat behind it looked to be somewhere close to Slocum's age, but carried herself like someone twice that age. Shallow wrinkles appeared at the corners of wizened eyes when she smiled and said, "Welcome to Whispering Hills."

"Looks like a fine place you have here," he said. "I'd like a room."

"Sorry, but we're booked up."

"Is it a holiday I don't know about?"

"No. We only have five rooms. One is the temporary residence of our town doctor and two are being rented by a family on their way to Missouri."

"Doesn't that leave two more rooms?"

"They're reserved."

Slocum felt his stomach twist in a way that was similar to the moments before he took a swing at a belligerent drunk. Although the woman wasn't as ugly or loud as someone who'd flopped onto the floor of a saloon, she was testing his patience all the same. "Look," he said in the most patient tone he could manage. "It's been a rough day. I need somewhere to sleep. I have money in my pocket. I'll pay for a room, and if the people with the reservations show up, we can talk about another arrangement."

"That never works out well," she said with a wince.

"This happens a lot?"

"We're the only hotel in town."

"The only hotel?"

She nodded. "Culbertson is a small town."

There was the twist again.

"How much to buy out that reservation?" Slocum asked.

She blinked and looked at him as if he'd just suggested murdering the family on their way to Missouri so he could sleep in one of their beds. "What are you talking about?"

"I'm asking how much money I can pay you to erase one of those reservations . . . just one . . . so I can have a room."

"I can't do that, sir. The reservation was made for Judge Whetuski."

"The judge needs two rooms?" Slocum asked.

"One for him. One for his clerk."

"His clerk?"

"Oh yes," the woman replied as if she was verifying the existence of her personal savior. "Judge Whetuski travels with a clerk that takes care of all his personal matters as well as his legal filing. Whenever he comes to town, he always requests two rooms. One for him and one for his clerk."

"Does one of those rooms have two beds in it?"

She didn't even need to think before nodding. "Of course. One is our suite. It has two beds and it's very beautiful. Catches the sun in the morning to warm up all four corners."

"Would it be possible for the judge to take that room so his clerk would still have a bed for himself?"

"Herself, actually. She's a delightful woman who's been working for Judge Whetuski for two years now."

"I imagine she's pretty."

"Oh yes. Delightful."

Not only did it grate against Slocum's nerves to be corrected in such a chipper tone by the increasingly maddening woman, but it made him wince to think of how good the odds were that the judge and clerk truly only used one room anyway and reserved the other for appearances. He drew a breath, which failed to calm him down, but he tried to keep up an appearance of his own as he asked, "Could the judge and clerk possibly take the room with two beds so I can rent the other room? I'd really appreciate it."

The woman's features took on a warmer hue and she curved her mouth as if she was looking down at a pitiful, wounded little puppy. "I know you would and I would love to accommodate you, but the judge always stays in two rooms. One for him and one for his clerk."

Resisting the urge to smash her desk into splinters before setting it on fire, he quietly turned his back to her and left the Whispering Hills Hotel.

12

Slocum approached the bar, found Slick behind it, and gripped the edge of the wooden surface as he snarled, "Give me another whiskey." A good portion of Slocum was hoping the balding man might shoot back with a smart comment, refuse him service, or do anything at all that would allow Slocum to unleash some of the aggravation that had built up in his system during his short time at Whispering Hills. Instead, the barkeep found a glass, filled it, and stood by with bottle in hand.

"Care for another?" Slick asked. "It's on the house."

"Frightened of that little lady, huh?"

"Nah. Well . . . maybe a touch. She was right in what she said, though. Without you here, that shooting could have been a lot worse. Apologies for my harsh tone before."

Since more liquor would only have added fuel to a fire that had dwindled on its own, Slocum said, "I'll pass on another drink, but thanks for the offer."

"The offer stands while you're in town." After starting to turn toward another customer, Slick wheeled back around and asked, "Will you be in town for very long?"

"Hopefully not."

That brought more joy to Slick's face than Slocum would have thought possible. "Then it stands. Welcome to Culbertson."

Slocum held on to his glass as he shifted to lean back against the bar. Bethany was talking with some men at a nearby card game and looked up within seconds after he'd spotted her. When she walked over to him, Slocum asked, "You're still here?"

"Not as a cook. I got roped into a card game being held later."

"I know how that goes. You ever have any luck at poker?"

"Not even a whiff of it."

"I know how that goes, too," he said. "Last game I lost wound up with me penniless and sleeping in front of a stable. Hopefully you fare a little better."

"Considering we're only playing for bragging rights and a few pennies, I'd say so. How'd you fare over at Whispering Hills?"

Not wanting to get into every frustrating detail, Slocum replied, "Every room's taken. Got another suggestion of where I might stay?"

"Sure. I live over on Third Avenue. It's not much of a walk from here. Of course, no two places within town limits is much of a walk from each other."

"I couldn't impose."

"Impose?" she scoffed. "You saved my life. Maybe you already forgot about that but I sure as hell haven't!"

"You already put some whiskey into my belly. That's more than enough payment as far as I'm concerned."

She narrowed her eyes and studied him with a playful squint.

"What's wrong with you?" he asked.

"I'm trying to figure out if you're playing at being modest or if you're angling for more."

"How about neither? We're even."

"Nope," she said with a definitive shake of her head. "That won't do it for me. I won't be able to look at myself in the mirror if I don't repay what you did. You need a place to stay and the Christian thing to do would be to put a roof over your head for the night. Seeing as how you saved my life, I should be doing a lot more." Bethany grabbed Slocum's hand and started dragging him away from the bar. "You're coming with me. Where's the rest of your things?"

"With my horse. I still need a place to put her up."

"I've got room for both of you at my house. Come along now."

Slocum went with her simply because Bethany didn't leave him much choice. She dragged him toward the front door as if she fully intended on tossing him through the broken window if he resisted. Before he got too far away, Slocum made sure Slick knew what to tell Daniel if he came to the Bullseye asking about his whereabouts.

Some old sheets had been hastily nailed over the window while Slocum had been at the sheriff's office. From the outside, light from the saloon gave the linen a warm glow that was pretty in a strange sort of way. At the very least, it was a peculiar sight in the middle of an otherwise sleepy town. Slocum collected his horse and led her by the reins while Bethany led him in a very similar manner. Culbertson wasn't completely dead. Some music was being played at another establishment farther down the street, and a few locals made their way from one building to another. A cart ambled past them on its way out of town, and the driver tipped his hat silently to everyone he passed.

"I imagine this is a far cry from Dodge City," she said.

"It sure is. Have you ever been there?"

"Once, but just to pass through. Most of my family is in the Dakotas, and I rarely get a chance to travel other than to see them."

"I suppose that could be a good thing. Never underestimate the comfort of a quiet town."

"Formerly quiet town," she corrected while also nudging him with her elbow. "Until you showed up."

"Yeah. Sorry about that. I gave you a chance to keep your distance, but you insisted I follow you home. Just remember that if things get noisy again."

They were walking past the Whispering Hills Hotel on their way to Virginia Avenue when Bethany closed the distance between her and Slocum. There hadn't been much distance in the first place, so now she was practically leaning against him. "If you play your cards right, things may get noisy again real soon."

Rather than try to think of anything to say to that, Slocum wrapped his arm around her shoulders and allowed her to guide him to the next street, which was Third. To the left and down a ways was a livery, but she steered him to the right, where several smaller buildings were clustered like blocky travelers huddling together for warmth. Those buildings were all little houses and cottages. Most of them were still and dark, but a few had windows that shone with a weak, flickering light cast by lanterns or candles within. Bethany's home was the last house in a row of four. From her front porch, he could see a good portion of the town. She brought him around to the back of her property, where he could see nothing but wide-open Kansas plains.

Motioning toward a small shelter built around a trough, she said, "I've got a horse as well, but she's a sweet old girl and shouldn't give yours any trouble. There's water in the trough and I have some oats for her to eat."

"That's very kind of you. I can take care of her right now if that's all right."

"It is. There's a pile of blankets in that bin," she added while pointing to a covered crate next to one used for feed. "When you're through, come inside."

"I will. And thanks again, Bethany. This is more than generous of you."

She waved him off while turning and walking back to the house.

Slocum wanted to watch her, but couldn't see much before she was swallowed up by the darkness. As the squeal of her door's hinges drifted through the air, he busied himself with getting the rented dun squared away within the shelter. There was a hitching post, the trough, and an old feed bag under there along with a tired gray horse that had barely moved apart from a few twitches of its ear or tail. "Mind some company tonight?" Slocum asked while tying the dun's reins to the post.

The other horse blinked lazily.

"Didn't think so. Are you hungry?"

Since Bethany's horse was more interested in being left alone, Slocum honored her wishes and fed his own. He then patted their necks and left them in peace.

It was a short walk to the house, and the back door was left open a crack for him as if he needed further incentive to step inside. There wasn't much light coming from the single lantern in the next room, but Slocum could tell he was in a small kitchen. "Bethany?" he called out. "Are you here?"

"Is the door shut?" she asked from deeper within the little house. "Sometimes it doesn't close all the way."

Slocum grinned and checked the door again. "It's shut now."

"Good. Come on in."

The next room was a little parlor that was even smaller than the kitchen. A narrow bookcase stretched up to within an inch of the ceiling. Two chairs were situated around a low, round table that wasn't much more than an oversized milking stool. A lantern hung on a hook between the bookcase and the front door. When Slocum first caught sight of another, much narrower doorway, he assumed it led to a closet. When Bethany peeked out from the upper corner of that doorway, he realized that must have been a staircase.

"You ready to settle in for the night?" she asked.

"I sincerely hope so."

"Good," Bethany said while coming down the rest of the stairs and walking through the narrow doorway. "Because I've got plans for you." She wore a simple nightgown that clung to her body and reached down to her ankles. The plain white cotton garment conformed to her figure to reveal rounded breasts with nipples that were already erect with anticipation and smooth, supple thighs. Her straw-colored hair hung freely in a tussle of curls around her face, and her eyes became wide as she quickened her pace to get to him.

Before Slocum had a chance to get a better look at her, Bethany had already wrapped her arms around him and pressed herself against him. She kissed him with a passion that grew each time their lips met. His hands went reflexively to her hips and found them to be firm and shapely. When he eased his touch up and down her body, he could tell she wasn't wearing anything apart from the nightgown.

"You . . . don't have to do this," he said when he could catch his breath.

Keeping her fingers laced together behind his neck, she leaned back just enough to look into his eyes. "Don't you want to?"

"It's not that. I just . . ."

His body responded to her closeness. The moment Slocum's erection strained against the front of his jeans, Bethany rubbed against it and smiled. "I can tell you want to."

"This is just something of a surprise."

"You didn't strike me as the bashful sort," she said with a touch of skepticism in her eyes.

Suddenly, Slocum didn't know what was holding him back. Perhaps it had been a long day or maybe he'd drunk too much whiskey, but whatever the reason for his hesitation, he was past it now. Slocum grabbed her hips tighter and pulled her close. She responded with a breathy moan and wrapped one leg around him so she could slide it along his thigh.

Every inch of her was warm and inviting. When Slocum buried his face against her neck, he was treated to the natural scent of her skin and the warmth of her breath against his ear.

"I could barely wait to get you here," she whispered. "As soon as I saw you again, I wanted you to fuck me good and hard."

"Well now," Slocum replied as he pulled back so he could unbuckle his gun belt and loosen his jeans. "I believe a lady should never be denied."

"I'm no lady," she told him. "And I sure as hell ain't gonna be denied."

She started unbuttoning his shirt and got about halfway done before Slocum had his pants down. His rigid cock ached to be inside her, and the notion that she was wearing nothing beneath her nightgown made him want her even more. Her fingers were still manipulating his shirt buttons when he turned her around and came up behind her. Bethany took his direction eagerly and grabbed the side of the bookcase as his hands moved around to cup her breasts. They were the perfect size to fill his hands, and she moaned appreciatively when he massaged them vigorously.

"I've had some thoughts about you, too," he said in a harsh tone directly into her ear.

She arched her spine as if responding on an animal level to his voice. "What have you been thinking?"

"How I wanted to get you in a spot just like this." He moved one hand away from her chest so he could begin gathering her nightgown. The fabric lifted up to reveal shapely legs and the creamy white flesh of her thighs. Once he had the nightgown rolled up over her hips, he moved his other hand down to hold it in place. Bethany was trembling with excitement by now and moved her feet into a wider stance.

"I can't wait anymore," she said while reaching down to hold her nightgown for him.

Slocum placed his left hand upon her hip, bent his knees, and used his right hand to guide the head of his penis between her legs. He found the wet lips of her pussy almost immediately and savored the moist feel of them gliding against his thick member. Bethany bent over a little more, held her breath, and remained still until he was there. Once he slid into her, they both exhaled gratefully.

"Damn," Bethany said as Slocum held on to both of her hips and started pumping. "Even better than I thought."

His only reply was to grab her tighter and pound into her with a single thrust that took her breath away. She clawed at the bookcase and arched her back as every inch of his rigid cock slid in and out of her.

Slocum reveled in the feel of her warm body and dripping pussy. Something about the sight of her was exciting on its own. A woman who stripped naked was one thing. A woman wrapped up in pretty clothes was another. Seeing a woman with her clothes rumpled up and gathered up to reveal her bare ass and legs was enough to make him grateful to be alive. There was no more banter or promises. Just a man and a woman seizing the moment to give in to their carnal desires. Slocum reveled in that even more by giving her backside a swat that sounded loudly throughout the room.

"Fuck me harder," she demanded.

He pounded into her a few times and slapped her hip again.

"Yes!" she cried. "Harder!"

He grabbed her with both hands and drove his cock into her again and again until she tossed her head back and let out a shuddering moan. When she was through, he pulled out and turned her around. Bethany followed his lead once more by moving where he wanted her to go and placing her shoulders against the wooden surface of her front door.

"You ain't through, are you?" she asked breathlessly.

"Not by a mile."

She smiled and hiked up her nightgown to once again reveal her bare thighs. As Slocum reached around and cupped her backside in both hands, she hopped up and wrapped her legs around his waist. Between his grip on her rump, her hands locked behind his neck, the firm hold of her legs wrapped around him, and her shoulders pressed against the door, Bethany remained in place so Slocum could once again enter her. His cock fit perfectly between her legs, sliding between her wet lips until he was buried solidly inside her.

"Oh my God," she said. "I don't think I ever want you to leave that spot."

"You don't want me to move?"

"I don't think so."

He rubbed her hips and slid slowly out of her so he could ease back in. "What about now?"

"All right," she said playfully. "You can move."

Slocum took that as his cue to begin pumping in and out. Bethany pressed her head against the door and closed her eyes as he drilled between her thighs. Her legs wrapped around him tightly and her fingernails began to dig into the flesh of his neck and shoulders. As he quickened his pace, Slocum tightened his grip on her buttocks. The smooth, firm curves felt good against his palms, and for the next several moments, it was as if she didn't weigh an ounce.

Just when Slocum thought he'd reached the pinnacle, he felt her start to grind her hips against him. The moment he slowed down to catch his breath, Bethany opened her eyes and went through a series of slow, circular motions. Soon, she found a spot that made his rigid shaft rub her in just the right way and her body started to tremble. From this angle, Slocum could feel her climax working its way from the base of her spine all the way to the tips of her toes. She arched her back and gripped him tightly. Despite his unwillingness to let her go, she loosened her legs and lowered them so she could stand on her own. That made it tough for Slocum to hold her, so he took a step back and allowed her to support herself. Before he could let out one frustrated word, she pushed him back a bit more so she had enough room to drop to her knees in front of him.

Bethany's hands brushed against his chest, and her lips grazed the front of his body from his stomach down to his erect penis. Keeping her hands flat against him, she maneuvered her lips to encircle the tip of his pole and slide all the way down its length. Her mouth felt good, but the touch of her tongue along the bottom of his shaft brought him right back to the point he'd reached a few moments ago.

"That's it," he said as he placed both hands upon the back of her head. "Just like that."

But she didn't need any instruction. As her hands wandered along the front of his body, her head bobbed back and forth so she could devour every inch of him. When she took him all the way into her mouth, she stayed put so her tongue could swirl around. Slocum held her in place and pushed himself in a little deeper, so she took him in that much farther and licked him faster.

Once Slocum's breath became quicker and shallower, she sucked him faster. The wet sound of him in her mouth drifted through the air, soon to be followed by his building moans. Her hair was soft between his fingers when he tightened his grip and exploded into her mouth. She remained in place for a few more seconds, licking him dry before finally leaning back.

"There now," she said with a naughty little smile. "Isn't that better than Whispering Hills?"

Slocum helped her to her feet and placed his hands upon her hips. "Depends on what type of room service they offer."

Bethany smacked his chest and groused for a little while, which did nothing to dim her enthusiasm when he peeled her nightgown off an hour later to enter her again.

13

It was two days before Judge Whetuski got to town. Slocum might have been angry with the wait if not for the fact that Bethany was more than happy to help him kill time. When she was cooking at the Bullseye, Slocum played cards or checked in on Sheriff Teaghan. When she wasn't working, Bethany couldn't keep her hands off him. She was a wild lover who somehow found a new way to surprise him every time she stripped Slocum out of his clothes. On the second day when he walked into the Whispering Hills Hotel, Slocum was almost as bowlegged as he would have been if he'd ridden into town from California in one stretch.

"Any word on if those rooms will be available?" he asked the woman behind the front desk. He wasn't interested in renting a room any longer, but it was the only way he could get her to say anything at all about whether or not the judge was in town. He may have been able to ask Sheriff Teaghan, but Slocum had quickly grown tired of seeing the apathetic lawman's face.

Still as vacant behind the eyes as the first time he'd seen her, she replied, "They're all filled up, Mr. Slocum."

"Filled? Not just reserved?"

"That's right. Judge Whetuski and his clerk arrived a few hours ago and they're settling in. That family should be leaving soon, though. Finally got their wagon fixed and fit for the rest of the ride into Missouri."

Slocum had stopped listening to her the moment she'd confirmed the judge was in town. "All right. Thanks." Upon leaving the Whispering Hills, he headed toward the sheriff's office on Virginia Avenue.

Teaghan's door was locked, and before Slocum could knock, the sheriff's single deputy shouted at him from the little jailhouse. "Nobody's to go in for a while. The sheriff wants it that way so he can talk to the judge in peace."

The deputy was a young man who looked even younger, owing to the lack of whiskers on his chin and the abundance of baby fat on his cheeks. In later years, it might have been a blessing to look so boyish. Now, it was hard for Slocum to take him seriously. "I'm part of the business they must be discussing," he said. "Doesn't that mean I get to have a word with them?"

"You'll wait for the trial just like anyone else."

"When will that be?"

The deputy was in mid-shrug when the front door of the sheriff's office was pulled open. Before the younger lawman could stop him, Slocum rushed to greet the sheriff as well as two others. One was a tall man who looked like a professor from a university back East. A well-tailored gray suit hung upon a narrow frame, and a clean-shaven face was accented by a pair of thick, round spectacles. A woman with dark hair and a pinched face wore clothes that seemed only slightly less expensive than the taller gentleman's. Slocum was surprised when she stepped up to intercept him before the sheriff could get to him.

"What is your business, sir?" she asked.

"I'm John Slocum. I'd like to have a word with the judge."

"Judge Whetuski's schedule is filled," she replied, speaking the judge's name as if it were connected to royalty. "If you'd like to make an appointment, you can speak to me."

The judge stopped a pace behind her and watched Slocum silently. Sheriff Teaghan finally managed to get past them both so he could shove Slocum toward the street. "What the hell do you think you're doing?" the sheriff asked. "This is a judge. You don't just strut up and start barking at him like you were in a saloon."

Although Slocum knew the lawman had a point, he wasn't about to bow to Teaghan just yet. Instead, he lowered his voice and took a less aggressive stance when he met the judge's gaze. "I'd just like to know what's going to happen with the matters that need to be resolved."

The judge responded well to Slocum's change in demeanor. Having ridden the legal circuit for any amount of time would have made him less of a starched shirt than a man accustomed to hearing cases in the lofty halls of a state's capitol. "If you're worried about the case involving you and those misinformed gunmen, I think it's fairly safe to say the matter should be resolved within the next day or two."

"That quick for a trial?"

"You'd rather wait longer?"

"No," Slocum said. "It just seemed that it would be dragged out more than that."

Judge Whetuski placed his hands upon the lapels of his suit coat and said, "I regret having to keep these good people waiting this long for me to arrive, especially when it's a matter that's already been handled by local peace officers."

"I'm not just talking about the broken window," Slocum said.

"Now that I'm here, I fully intend on seeing all of these unfortunate matters through to their proper conclusion."

"And what about the men that were brought here?" Slocum asked.

When the judge didn't respond right away, the sheriff explained, "He means the men being held in the jailhouse."

"Are you involved with that Misty Creek case, Mr. Slocum?" the clerk asked.

"I helped bring the men in," he replied. "And since it wasn't long after that when I was shot at to try and get me to leave town, I'd say I'm hip-deep involved in it."

After sifting through a batch of papers that she'd been holding as if they were a newborn baby, the clerk looked over to Judge Whetuski and shook her head. "Do you have proof that these two cases are connected, Mr. Slocum?" Judge Whetuski asked.

"The men who shot at me wanted me to get out of town. Apart from taking up space while I was eating pork chops, I can't think of any other reason they might have for doing something like that."

"I was told that was a case of mistaken identity."

"That's bullshit." Seeing the angry glint in the corner of the judge's eye, Slocum added, "Sir."

"I intend on questioning them shortly," Whetuski said in a voice that had suddenly acquired several layers of frost. "Until then, you'll have to excuse me. Sheriff . . ."

"Teaghan," the lawman said with an embarrassed scowl.

"Sheriff Teaghan will let you know when the trial is to commence." After that, the judge, his clerk, and Teaghan all formed a procession that led to the jailhouse. Whetuski stepped to one side so the lawman could unlock the jail's door and hold it open for him like a coachman deferring to a lord.

"Let me guess," Slocum said to the deputy, who was the only one left behind with him. "That judge is running for some sort of political office."

"Senator," the deputy replied.

"Sounds about right."

Stabbing a finger at him, the deputy said, "You steer clear of them until you're called for. Understand?"

"Of course," Slocum replied while holding his hands up. "He is a judge after all."

The deputy was surprised by the ease with which Slocum had complied and did a poor job of showing it. His single nod and attempt at gruffness when he headed back toward the office were almost enough to make Slocum smile. "Stay in town and wait to hear about the trial. If you try to leave before then—"

Slocum turned his back to the younger man and walked away. "I know the rest."

This wasn't Slocum's first time dealing with a judge. This being a legal matter, he knew better than to hold his breath while waiting for anything to be resolved in anything close to a reasonable amount of time. Therefore, he figured he had enough time to get involved in one of Bethany's penny-ante card games. There was one other saloon in town with much higher poker stakes, but Slocum was still feeling the ill effects of his last loss and wasn't about to make things worse by risking another one. When a man felt his luck was that bad, it was always better to pay heed and cool his heels with some other diversion.

He'd barely gotten a feel for the game when Slocum was interrupted by a tap on his shoulder. Looking up from the expectant faces of the old men sitting at the table with him, he found the Bullseye's barkeep staring down at him. "What is it, Slick?" Slocum asked.

"Someone to see you."

"Tell her I'll be along once I break even."

"Not Bethany," Slick replied. "He's waiting out back."

Slocum sat up straight and lowered his voice so it wouldn't carry to the other small-time gamblers and locals who'd come in for the dinner special. "Did he give a name?"

"No, just that I was to tell you to meet him around back."

After making some hasty apologies, Slocum gathered up the four dollars he'd won and walked out. He watched the street every step of the way as he walked down the alley that took him to the lot behind the Bullseye, making sure never to offer his back to anyone posted in the building across the street. When he saw Daniel leaning against the back wall of the Bullseye, Slocum asked, "Where the hell have you been?"

"Like I told you before. I wanted to meet up with another one of the men trying to bring these assholes to justice. Cullen."

"Did you find him?"

"Yeah, and he wants to meet you."

"Better be soon because the judge is in town."

"I know."

Slocum drew a deep breath and let it out like it was steam. "You've been keeping an eye on things here?"

"Yeah. I was a scout, remember? That's what I'm trained to do."

"Why didn't you at least keep me posted?"

"Because if anyone's watching you," Daniel explained, "they would have seen me coming in to tell you what's what. And if those men don't get any reason to believe I may be nearby, that makes it all the easier to watch where they go."

"One flaw in that logic," Slocum pointed out. "I can tell you where they went. The jailhouse right next to the shitter behind the sheriff's office after being patched up by the doctor."

"Not all of them," Daniel replied with a sly grin.

"You found the one that got away?"

Daniel nodded. "Caught sight of him skulking around trying to catch you with your back turned."

"When was that?"

"The other night when that saloon girl took you back to her house."

"You saw that, too?" Slocum asked.

"And heard it." When Slocum tried to look as if he didn't know what he was talking about, Daniel raised an eyebrow and said, "Oh yes, I heard it. Don't try to tell me that was the birds screaming like that."

"Oh, for Christ's sake. Are you a scout or a Peeping Tom?"

"That fella who was trying to get the drop on you almost was the Peeping Tom. That is, before I made him realize he wasn't as sneaky as he thought. I made some noise like I was walking to one of them other houses south of Main Street and that was enough to chase him away."

"Did you find out who he is? A name?"

"Arthur Vesper. Does it ring a bell?"

Slocum thought about it for a moment and sighed, "No. How'd you find out who he was?"

"I recognized his face. Are you familiar with vigilante groups?"

"Not in this neck of the woods. Is Arthur Vesper a vigilante?"

"Yeah," Daniel said. "At least that's what he calls himself. He did some work in the Dakotas after getting his start in Nebraska. I've heard the name more than once ever since me and Cullen started riding through these parts. Vesper's become a rich man clearing out land for the railroads, ranchers, or anyone else with enough money to pay his fees."

"Clearing land of what?" Slocum asked, although he already dreaded hearing the answer.

"Settlers too stubborn to accept payment to surrender their property. Business owners who refuse to allow their stores to be knocked down so tracks can be laid down. Most anyone who stands in the way of what some might consider to be progress." Daniel closed his eyes and then opened them as if he couldn't bear to watch what flashed through his mind. "More recently, he's been taking government money to spill Indian blood."

"Why's the government paying him to do that?"

Daniel gave him a slow, sorrowful shrug. "Plenty of reasons if you're so inclined. Some may want to silence tribe members who threaten to fight for patches of land. Some could want to convince a tribe to move for some project or another. Major Garrison would have done it to clear out his workload and make it look like he was doing something with his command other than stealing supplies and such from the quartermaster and selling them off."

"You think that's what happened at Misty Creek?"

"Garrison was known to make a profit where he could when his commanders weren't looking, but Misty Creek was a whole different animal. Cullen learned something about it, which is why he wants to meet you as soon as possible."

"Can't you just tell me?" Slocum asked.

"I could, but Cullen's ridden with me for a good long while. He wants to meet the outsider I'm bringing into this affair before he's brought in any further and I'm honoring that request. Besides, Cullen is a good man and a damn fine marksman. Having him on our side without any reservations will work out best all around."

Since Slocum wasn't about to argue with logic that held loyalty and friendship in such high regard, he said, "I just need to get my horse and we can go. When was the last time you saw Vesper?"

"About an hour ago. He was settling in for the night."

"You're sure he's not keeping an eye on me? He did find me once and was only a few inches off when he decided to fire a shot at me."

"He wasn't off," Daniel said. "He told you he wanted to try and run you out of town, and that seems to be exactly what he did. From what I've heard about the man, Vesper is meticulous and calculating. If he'd wanted you dead, things would have gone a lot differently at that saloon."

14

Culbertson was a small enough town that the light coming from its windows barely made a dent in the darkness of a nighttime sky. Upon riding beyond town limits, however, Slocum was wrapped in a gloom that was almost palpable. He allowed his horse to move at her own pace until his eyes adjusted. Once they did, he was treated to the dim glow of a partial moon as well as the pinprick brilliance of countless stars splashed over his head. He was still in Kansas, after all, which meant the trail leading to Cullen's camp was mostly flat and uneventful.

Daniel rode ahead at a quicker pace, but not quick enough for Slocum to lose sight of him. Rather than use a hand signal that might go unseen, he let out a sharp whistle when he wanted Slocum to come to a stop. "Cullen," he said in a voice that seemed to carry for miles in the dark expanse of open ground. "That you?"

The scout's eyes were definitely sharper than Slocum's. If not for Daniel, he may very well have kept riding without spotting the little flicker of light ten yards or so from the trail.

"Who's that with you?" a disembodied voice asked from the darkness.

"It's that man I told you about earlier. John Slocum."

"Let's get a look at him."

Slocum could see Daniel well enough to know the scout had turned toward him, but wasn't sure what to do from there. Daniel motioned for him to come forward and Slocum obliged, albeit grudgingly. "We rode all the way out here," Slocum grumbled. "Your friend is dug in deeper than a tick and already recognizes you. Why the hell do we still have to go through this sneaking nonsense?"

"Because that's how we've stayed alive this long," Daniel said. "Now just come up alongside me so Cullen can get a look."

Once he rode up to Daniel's side, he held his arms out as if submitting to a search. After a few silent moments, he heard the rustle of footsteps. They didn't come from the dim light of the sputtering campfire, but cracked against the dry ground five or six yards directly in front of and to the right of Slocum's position.

"You're John Slocum?"

After squinting and focusing on that patch of nearby ground, Slocum could make out the figure of a man in the shadows. He wore dark clothes and a hat that was large enough to make his head blend in with the other dark blobs in his field of vision. "I am."

"Danny tells me you've done a good job of standing by him this far."

"Seemed like the proper thing to do considering the job he's taken on."

"Sometimes proper ain't an easy thing to do," the shadow said.

"You don't have to tell that to me. I've lost count of how many times I've nearly gotten myself killed by taking action instead of listening to my common sense and hanging back where it's safe."

The figure took another couple of steps forward and removed the floppy, wide-brimmed hat that had done such a good job of obscuring his face. He looked to be several years older than Daniel with the wrinkles and scars to show for it. Despite all of that weariness and dirt that had been smeared onto his cheeks and chin, he found enough in him to place a friendly smile on his face as he extended his hand to Slocum.

"Seems like losing any hint of common sense is what makes men like us do what we do," Cullen said. "Glad to have another crazy man riding with us."

Even after all the trouble of a night ride and being dragged around through an excessive amount of dramatics involving secret meetings and hiding in the dark, Slocum couldn't help but grin. He reached down from atop his horse, shook Cullen's hand, and wasn't surprised to feel a strong, confident grip from the other man.

"Now that we've got all of the introductions out of the way, would you mind letting me know why I'm out here in the middle of the night instead of having a hot meal near a fire?"

Cullen nodded as a shot cracked through the air to snap his head to one side. Slocum was still gripping the other man's hand as Cullen fell sideways and swung into the legs of Slocum's horse. The impact came as a result of the velocity of the shot that had bored through Cullen's skull and the angle from which he hung from Slocum's hand. Even though the man had become deadweight, Slocum was reluctant to let him go until he could swing Cullen away so he wouldn't get trampled by the frightened dun.

"The shot came from that direction," Slocum said as he pointed to the north. Even though he couldn't see much of anything over there, he trusted his ears enough to have faith in his statement.

Daniel had pulled the rifle from its boot as soon as he'd swung down from the saddle. He dropped to one knee, brought the rifle to his shoulder, and levered in a round. "Ride toward the camp and see if you can draw his fire," the scout said in a harsh whisper. "Just be careful."

Slocum drew his .44 and leaned forward over his horse's neck. The dun wanted to get moving and responded as soon as it felt the snapping reins. Another shot cracked through the air, but wasn't accompanied by the hiss of a bullet. That struck Slocum as peculiar, but he didn't have time to dwell on it before another round whipped past his head. Whoever was pulling that trigger was a long ways off and the shots that had been taken since Cullen was hit were in a meandering pattern.

The dun carried Slocum toward the dim glow of a little campfire that was mostly hidden by a tall ring of rocks and branches. Smoke rose from that spot like a wraith being drawn up toward the stars. Slocum fired once in the general direction of the sniper, which was answered by the crack of a round speeding about ten yards off its mark. Considering how dead-on the first shot had been, the seemingly random pattern didn't make any sense. Unless . . .

"Down!" Slocum shouted as he followed his own advice by swinging from his saddle to hit the ground in a heap. His dun was still shaken, but wasn't about to bolt or rear up just from losing her rider.

Daniel was already down as far as he could go without losing his line of sight to the distant shooter's assumed position. He crouched in a one-knee stance with his rifle held so his left hand was drawn in close to the trigger guard. That gave him a steadier aim for long-range shots, but was a notoriously bad decision if the target was moving. He fired, levered in another round, and glared over the top of his barrel. "Almost got him," he said in a voice that Slocum could barely hear.

"Get down, damn it!" Slocum said.

Another shot hissed toward them after a pause that was

longer than the ones between the last few shots that had come at them from the distant shadows.

"You hear me?" Slocum asked as he scampered toward Daniel while keeping the lowest profile possible. "He's trying to sight in on us. He must have picked up Cullen near the campfire and zeroed in when he stepped out to shake my hand. Whoever that sniper is, he's doing the same thing we were trying to do. Getting us to move and shoot so he could pick another target."

Slocum spoke in a torrent that flowed out of him until he reached Daniel's side. Once there, he didn't see any hint that his words had had any effect. The scout still held his rifle while kneeling over Cullen's body and glaring toward the north. Then, he simply fell over.

"Shit!" Slocum grunted when he saw the small dark hole in Daniel's face created by a round that had punched through his skull between his left eye and the bridge of his nose.

Daniel's expression remained focused even though his eyes were glazed over. If they saw anything any longer, it was the face of his Maker.

Now that both scouts were dead, Slocum forced himself to think only of survival. Whether or not the marksman was Arthur Vesper didn't matter. Slocum's only concern was that the other man's eye was sharp enough to pick off two men in the dark from possibly a hundred yards away.

The shots had stopped for now, but that didn't make Slocum feel any better since the horses were the only ones presenting any sort of target at the moment. Slocum's eyes were picking up a bit more now. He fixed them upon his horse and made his way toward her.

"Ride away!" a distant voice said as if it had somehow intercepted Slocum's subtle movements. "Ride away and don't come back! They're dead! You're next!"

The words rolled in from the distance like an approaching storm. Slocum didn't process them for meaning so much as to try and pinpoint the location of their source. As far as he could tell, the marksman was still north of his position and maybe a little closer than he'd previously guessed. Slocum mulled through those bits of information while crawling toward his horse. Once Slocum got close enough to reach out and pat the dun's side, he calmed the horse down while coiling his body like a spring. It was time to start doing some pinpointing of his own. "What's the matter?" he shouted. "Too yellow to fight unless you can do it from a distance?"

For a moment, Slocum thought the man in the shadows wasn't going to take the bait. He waited patiently, crouching beside his dun, steadying the animal and praying his taunt was eating away at the marksman's soul. Feeling that the fuse was burning close to the powder keg, Slocum added, "Guess you'd prefer me to present a bigger target. Maybe one as big as a window covering a room full of unarmed people?"

The explosion came in the form of a voice that sounded more like the angry howl of a wolf. "You're too stupid to know how lucky you are! The only reason you weren't killed already is because you ain't directly involved in this matter. If you want that to change, you'll be stretched out like those two men at your feet right now!"

If the marksman thought Slocum was still by Daniel's and Cullen's bodies, perhaps Slocum's crawl had been worth the indignity. Also, the angry words rolling in from the north were loud enough to take a better guess at where the marksman might be hiding. It was time to take another gamble because Slocum knew staying put for much longer would only buy him a wound to match the ones that were given to both dead scouts.

In one smooth motion, Slocum pulled himself up using his grip on the saddle, stuck a foot into a stirrup, and climbed onto the dun's back. He didn't waste any time in getting settled before snapping the reins and tapping his heels against her sides. The horse was all too ready to get moving and charged toward the north. He hadn't ridden for more than four steps before Slocum pulled on the reins to steer the horse sharply to the left. He lowered his head, went a bit farther, and then veered to the right. Although the first turn hadn't done much more than frustrate his horse, the second put him out of the path of a shot that was fired from the shadows ahead. Slocum grinned at the prospect of finally taking the fight to the sniper and charged onward.

The shots that came at him now were very different than the ones that had hissed randomly through the air before Daniel had gone down. Some blazed a path through the air that was a foot or two away from Slocum while others got close enough to send a chill beneath his skin as if that part of his body fully expected to be perforated.

Slocum didn't fire at the hidden marksman. Since he figured the killer wasn't about to be rattled by gunshots pointed in his direction, wasting ammunition that way could very well prove to be a fatal error. When it came to dealing with men like this one, a single mistake was often enough to cross the line between being alive or dead. All of this rushed through Slocum's mind as he drew closer to where he'd guessed the marksman might be hiding. He paused long enough to take a look at the rustling grass and swaying bushes, but wasn't about to present an easy target. When he got moving again, Slocum tapped the dun's sides in a way that made the horse lunge forward. His best chance at avoiding the marksman's next bullet was to keep moving as quickly and unpredictably as possible. From what he knew about sharpshooters, their style usually didn't lend itself to up-close battles, but Slocum wasn't about to bet his life on that.

When Slocum veered to the right and then right again, a shot blasted from a spot about ten to twelve yards behind him. The bullet went wide, probably because the marksman had banked on Slocum following a similar zigzag course that had brought him this far. Instead, Slocum brought the horse around while raising his .44 to sight along the top of its barrel. Whenever a shot presented itself, he would have to make it count.

A mist hung in the air nearby, curling lazily without much of a breeze to stir it. He climbed down from the saddle while searching the darkness any way he could. The .44 twitched toward every sound without finding anything more than a restless animal or branch that had been loosed by the wind.

A few more cautious steps brought Slocum close enough to the mist to identify it as burnt gunpowder. The marksman was close. That realization made Slocum anxious and nervous at the same time. Both he and the marksman were prepared to seize even the smallest opportunity to send the other to hell.

Slocum wanted to say something to try and draw the marksman out, but that would only give away his own position. He also wanted to keep still so he could better take in his surroundings and pick out anything that might be out of place. Unfortunately, that would also make it that much easier for the marksman to pick him out from the rest of the shadows. So Slocum stayed low, remained silent, and kept moving.

While creeping in an arcing back-and-forth pattern, he kept his boots less than an inch above the ground at the highest point of any step. He barely noticed the constant drone of insects behind him until it suddenly stopped.

At that same moment, his boot tapped against something solid that was lying in the grass to his left. His finger tensed upon his trigger and his muscles strained to turn him toward the thing he'd discovered without disturbing enough of his surroundings to make a noise. Whatever his boot had found was thicker and heavier than a branch and much smaller than a log. It seemed too narrow and smooth to be a rock, but that was about all Slocum could gather from sliding his foot along the object's side. He stood there for another couple of seconds, poised to fight for his life at the drop of a hat.

The stink of gunpowder caked the inside of his nose.

His ears still rang from the shots that had been fired, and his eyes strained to see whatever could be waiting for him in any one of a thousand shifting shadows.

Something rustled through branches at least fifty to sixty yards away. Slocum crouched and extended his gun hand in front of him. The moonlight cast its dim, milky glow upon the polished iron until every nick in its surface was visible to him. He held his breath to better hear anything around him. Although the rustling was getting louder, he knew he couldn't move toward it quickly enough to catch whatever was making the sound before it had a chance to get away. And since he knew the marksman needed only one good chance to put a round through his head, Slocum couldn't afford to blindly charge through unfamiliar terrain like a fool.

Like a reflection on rippling water that finally coalesced into a picture, the rustling sounds became recognizable as footsteps. Although he couldn't rule out the prospect of the marksman having an accomplice, he doubted another shooter would have been kept a secret for so long. That, as well as simple gut-level instinct, told Slocum that the marksman had gotten away. A moment after reaching for the object he'd tapped with his boot, he knew what it was. Suppressing the urge to swear out loud, Slocum picked up the rifle and moved his fingers along its barrel. The weapon was still warm from being fired, which meant the marksman had most likely ditched it in favor of another rifle so he didn't waste time to reload before moving along. It was a damn waste of a weapon, so Slocum picked it up and propped it over his shoulder.

The sound of distant footsteps shifted into the thump of hooves against the packed soil. Knowing he couldn't make it back to his horse fast enough to overcome the other man's head start, Slocum stood his ground to see if the marksman might circle back around. Unfortunately, he didn't. While making the walk back to his rented dun, Slocum vowed to put that discarded rifle to good use.

15

The first part of the next day was spent with an undertaker who was one of the jolliest men Slocum had met in a long time. He wore the standard black suit and starched white shirt that might have been a uniform for men in his line of work, but his pudgy, rose-colored cheeks never once lost their gleeful expression. When Slocum approached the undertaker in his parlor, he was greeted with a warm smile and a firm handshake. "Mark Krispin," the gravedigger said. "Pleased to meet ya!"

When the undertaker was told about the job he was to do, his eyes reflected heartfelt warmth and genuine compassion. "Oh my lord," Krispin said. "Two men were killed?"

"That's right."

"I didn't hear about it."

"That's because it happened outside of town," Slocum replied. "I've already told the sheriff about it, so I'd like it if it wasn't made into today's gossip." That last part was something of a bent truth since Slocum hadn't seen the sheriff just yet, but Teaghan was going to hear all about it.

"You can count on me being absolutely discreet," the

135

undertaker said. "Although I must admit it is unusual the sheriff didn't approach me first."

"He usually comes to you regarding all the deaths in or out of town?"

"The shooting deaths, yes. Although," the jolly man added with a shrug, "there really haven't been that many. Considering all the commotion around Judge Whetuski being here, I suppose it isn't so strange that I wouldn't hear from the sheriff."

"The judge usually kicks up some dust, huh?"

"You could say that. No matter how petty they are, all the legal matters that have been stewing for however long it's been since his last visit are always about to boil over by the time he arrives. This time is something special, like a big pot of steamy . . ."

Guessing the undertaker was looking for another food to reference, Slocum offered, "Soup?"

"Yes!" he said while clapping his hands over his belly. "A big kettle of boiling soup that's been cooking ever since those killers were brought into the jailhouse. Although I should wait to hear what the decision is before I call them something like that."

"Right," Slocum said while suppressing the urge to pass a few judgments of his own. "So what can you do for these two men outside of town? If possible, I'd like to bury them somewhere close to where they fell."

"Do they have any family?"

"I'll look into it. Just keep in mind," Slocum said, "they were military men."

The undertaker squinted and asked, "Are you requesting a color guard or some sort of honors?"

"Just make sure they're buried with respect and a proper marker befitting men who served their country."

"Oh, rest assured, they will be treated well. If you can tell me their approximate measurements and show me where they are, I can bring them back here and make sure they're—"

"No," Slocum snapped. Considering the things that might be said about them at the upcoming trial, Slocum didn't want to take a chance of Daniel's and Cullen's deaths being treated like a circus or an excuse to drag their names through the mud for a murderous Army officer to divert some unkind attention toward men who could no longer defend themselves. The scouts had done their part and should be granted a peaceful end. "They're going to be laid to rest outside of town and it's going to be right now. If it's extra, just tack it on to the bill." He then proceeded to give a short description of the two dead men.

"All right. I already have some coffins made as well as a cart. I'm assuming there's not to be a service."

"That's right."

The undertaker shrugged and went about his preparations as if he were fixing up the lunch he was so obviously craving. Slocum lent a hand where it was needed, and soon they were both on their way back out to the spot where Daniel and Cullen had been killed. Every step of the way, Slocum kept his eyes open for anyone that might be following or watching too closely. Apart from the typical glances an undertaker with a load of coffins might get, there was nothing alarming in the reactions of any of the locals.

Slocum showed the undertaker to the field, which looked vastly different in the light of day. Instead of shadows concealing any number of hiding spots, there were only weeds, scattered trees, and bushes collected in clusters here and there. Upon seeing the bodies, Krispin took some measurements and nodded in approval.

"Just like you described," the other man said. "Or close enough anyway. The coffins I brought should do just fine. Given some more time, I could craft something much more special for your departed friends."

"No, this will be fine."

Surveying the quiet field, the undertaker mused, "Yes, this will be fine. Very restful. A tranquil place to rest after what must have been tumultuous lives."

With seemingly nothing else to catch his eye at the moment, Slocum decided to put the undertaker to work in another capacity. "Need any help with that?" he asked.

"If you don't mind," the undertaker replied. He stood at Daniel's head and Slocum grabbed his feet so the two men could lift the body up and lower it into the first coffin. After that, Cullen was similarly contained and the undertaker committed himself to the task of digging. He swung the shovel with the same amount of gusto as a man who received top pay for driving railroad spikes. This time, when Slocum offered to help, the undertaker politely refused. "My previous employment was digging drainage and irrigation ditches with my father," he explained. "So quite honestly I could probably do this job faster without you."

Slocum nodded and looked around as if he were doing nothing more than taking in the scenery. From his vantage point atop his horse, he could see where the marksman had probably been hiding as well as the route he must have taken to make his escape. It didn't take a master planner to pull off what the sniper had done. A little forethought and some rudimentary knowledge of the land would have sufficed. "You seem to know a lot about what goes on in town."

"I sure do."

"I'd guess you know pretty much everyone who lives here."

"Part of my job, as you might guess. Everyone who lives here could very well die here." Suddenly, Krispin stopped what he was doing so he could look directly up at Slocum. For the first time, his expression soured. "That must seem awfully callous to say. Please don't think I make light of what I do."

"Sometimes we all have to make light of what we do,"

Slocum replied. "Otherwise a lot of us would go bat shit loco."

The undertaker chuckled, but not too loudly. Even with his jovial manner, he never once lost the respectful air that ran beneath everything he'd done from the moment he'd gotten to within sight of the bodies. He may not have been dour, but he wasn't about to dishonor the souls he'd come to lay to rest.

"Ever heard of someone named Vesper?" Slocum asked. While the question felt like a rock being dropped onto an otherwise quiet pond, he couldn't think of a better way to get it out there. Fortunately, the undertaker didn't seem to mind.

Krispin stuck the blade of the shovel into the ground and cocked his head. "That does sound familiar although I can't say as I've ever met him."

"What have you heard?"

"What sort of thing are you looking for?"

Thanks to how well the conversation had gone this far, the undertaker didn't seem overly concerned with Slocum's questions. However, it wouldn't take much for that to change. Slocum kept his voice easygoing while doing his best to skirt some potentially thin ice. "I heard that name mentioned in the Bullseye. Sounded like he was a pretty important fellow here in town. I've been looking for work, so I could use all the important friends I can make."

In any saloon, there was a good bet that over half of the locals in town could be mentioned over drinks either as the source of a complaint or in connection to a debt. As for looking for work, that was another sort of thing that sounded direct but could mean any number of things or nothing at all. At any rate, the undertaker didn't give it much thought before replying, "Come to think of it, I have heard of an Arthur Vesper. The sheriff mentioned him while I was discussing a burial with his deputy."

"What burial?"

"Oh, it was a messy affair. If this town had a newspaper, I imagine it would have been splashed all over the front page. A pair of Indian fellas rode in to start trouble and Mr. Vesper chased them off. One was killed, which is what I was speaking to the deputy about."

"And the other?" Slocum asked.

"Don't know. Got away, I suppose. If he was locked up, I imagine I would have heard about it. Last time Sheriff Teaghan had an Indian in his jail, the whole town rallied to string him up."

"Why?"

"More messy business, I'm afraid. The Proctor family was one of the founders of Culbertson, and the only reason they stayed here instead of moving on to California to pursue their original plan was on account of losing their wagon master and supplies to an Indian attack. Folks come here from other parts of Kansas, Nebraska, or Wyoming, and there's no shortage of sad stories involving the red man in any of those places." Now that the undertaker had almost finished with one grave, he was more than happy to keep talking while starting the other. "I put that dead Indian into a potter's field a mile outside of town and that was the last of it. Frankly, I was glad to hear the end of such nasty talk."

"Why did Vesper chase the Indians out?" Slocum asked.

"Don't know. I just heard his name mentioned by the sheriff is all. I could ask him if you like."

"No need for that. Any idea where I might find him?"

"The sheriff?"

"No," Slocum said in a patiently measured tone. "Arthur Vesper."

"Oh, I believe he lives down on Third Avenue south of Main."

"You wouldn't happen to know which house, would you? If I could speak to him about this business opportunity, it could benefit both of us."

Business opportunity was another simple term that folks

could interpret in any number of important ways. Whichever one the undertaker chose, it was enough to get him to say, "There are only three houses along that stretch. One of them belongs to Johann Proctor. That's easy enough to pick out. Another might still be empty after Sarah Trapp left, and the third is Vesper's."

"Are you sure about that?"

"More or less. He and the sheriff were discussing something, and Mr. Vesper wanted to talk more at his house down on South Third. The rest is as I said."

Slocum wasn't sure if the information would be enough for him to find Vesper right away, but it was a hell of a lot more than he'd had a minute ago. One thing he definitely took away from the conversation was to watch what he said in the presence of undertakers. If they were all like this one, they enjoyed town gossip more than an entire sewing circle of nosy old women.

They engaged in some more small talk before the undertaker accepted any more of Slocum's help to lower the coffins into the graves. When it was time to cover them, Mark picked up the shovel and said, "Any thoughts on the markers?"

"Nothing fancy. Just a simple blessing."

"I've sent plenty of military men to their final rest, so I'm certain I can put together something. Is . . . umm . . . is price an object?"

"Just make it look nice. I want their names carved in stone and the grave easy enough to find if any family members come looking to pay their respects."

"In that regard, you just tell any family they have to talk to me. I'll bring them out here personally."

Slocum didn't doubt that for a second. He also wasn't sure how he'd pay that bill but knew he'd come up with something. "You're a good man, Mark. You've been a big help."

"Just doing my job. Where should I send the bill?"

"I can be found at the Bullseye. You know where that is?"

"Of course! I prefer the beer at the Wilfred Arms on Virginia, but that's just me. You should see it in a day or two."

Slocum parted ways with the undertaker, knowing full well that both scouts were in good hands.

16

Finding Arthur Vesper's home was a simple matter of following the directions Slocum had been given. Just as the undertaker had described, there were three houses built on Third Street south of Main. The first one looked empty, and upon a few quick peeks through some of the windows, Slocum verified that it was. The next one was large enough to be Culbertson's town hall. He walked past it just as the back door opened to allow an old woman and three small children to spill outside. Judging by the sprawl of the property and the number of generations under one roof, he figured that was the Proctor home. That left one smaller house at the end of the row.

If Slocum was a killer looking to stay in town without exposing himself to attack or limiting his options for escape, that was the house he would have chosen. Like Bethany's place, half of its windows looked out to open land. A fence was built up around it and most of the windows were shuttered. When the small children were distracting the old woman enough, Slocum moved past them and ducked around the shuttered house, hopped the fence, and looked

143

for a way inside. Part of him hoped the owner would be away so he could get in and have a look without being interrupted. Another part wanted Vesper to be home so he could be there to catch a bullet to the heart as payback for killing Daniel and Cullen. Before any of that took place, however, Slocum needed to make certain he was going after the right man.

He knew better than to try the doors. Not only would a man on his guard keep them locked, but they were visible from the Proctor house next door. It had gotten warmer over the last few days. Not as bad as Kansas in the dead of summer, but warm enough to make someone sweat while cooped up inside. No killer's blood was cold enough to see him through that, so Slocum began testing the windows around the sides of the house that looked out to nothing but flat terrain. Sure enough, he found one that the home's owner had opened and forgotten to latch. Slocum slid the window up, climbed inside, and eased it down again. When he looked for the latch, all he found were matching sections of splintered wood on the window's frame and pane.

The interior of the house was quiet. Slocum crouched in a sparsely furnished bedroom with his hand resting upon the holstered .44 just as he'd done when he'd been waiting for the marksman to take his next shot the night before. No shot came. Not even a board creaked. After giving it another few moments, Slocum thought his luck may have taken a turn for the better and he'd arrived while Vesper was away. Now his search could begin. The only problem was that he didn't know exactly what he was looking for. Even when digging for a needle in a haystack, a man knew what the needle looked like. Time wasn't on his side so he began working his way through the house and hoped for the best.

It was a small, two-story home. Most of the rooms on the first floor were close to empty. There were chairs, a bed or two, and some random personal things scattered about like shoes, some books, and a pair of spectacles. The kitchen was stocked with bare essentials, which amounted to a whole lot of canned fruits, beans, and other supplies that someone would eat while on the trail as opposed to being at home.

"No woman's touch, that's for certain," Slocum said as he closed a cabinet near a small stove.

Upstairs was a different matter. There were only two rooms, but it was plain to see they were where Vesper spent most of his time. One was a bedroom filled with clothes, more books, and trunks. The other was a study containing a large desk and so many pictures hanging about that Slocum doubted he could find one patch of empty wall bigger than his hand. Most of the pictures showed the same man, a balding figure with sunken cheeks and a hawk nose. Dark, narrowed eyes betrayed a wicked soul, even in the photographs where the mouth beneath them was curved into a smile. The photographs were predominantly of men in military uniforms. Slocum counted at least a dozen Army generals pictured with their arm draped over the hawk-nosed fellow's shoulder at the site of one victory or another. There was even a picture of that man standing in a row of three others shaking hands with a former President.

Photographs weren't the only things framed and hanging upon the wall. There were several medals, ribbons, and pins that had either once been on a uniform or presented to Vesper for one reason or another. Slocum got closer to the wall so he could read the words engraved on some of the placards or the medals themselves.

"Outstanding marksmanship, courage under fire, valor, more outstanding marksmanship, and a few for performing above and beyond while in combat." Slocum let out a slow whistle and added, "Looks like I've found my sniper."

Although that revelation made plenty of sense, it still didn't set right with him. Any man who'd earned those medals and had such an outstanding career in the Army could have made the shots that he'd witnessed. What rubbed him the wrong way was that the same man had become a cold-blooded murderer responsible for the deaths of two former Army scouts.

His eyes darted about the room, looking for anything that might fill in some more gaps. He found several rifles of varying caliber and model, which once again fit if Vesper was the shooter who'd taken down Cullen and Daniel. During a quick search of the upstairs bedroom, Slocum also found a large strongbox nestled at the bottom of a closet. Inside the reinforced iron container was money stacked neater than if it were in a bank vault. Before he could get much of an idea of how much was there, he heard a door swing open downstairs.

Going by the heavy sound of the footsteps, there were at least two men coming inside. Having seen the sparseness of the lower rooms, Slocum knew any careless movement that was made upstairs would more than likely echo in the rooms below. Whether that was by design or happenstance, it posed one hell of a problem for him now.

After the footsteps had made their way to the vicinity of the kitchen, a gruff voice drifted through the house. Fortunately, the sparseness of the lower level also made it easier for Slocum to hear what was being said.

"The trial is tomorrow," the gruff voice declared. "Tell me you've done the job I paid you for."

The other voice had a sharper, slightly nasal edge to it and was also the same voice Slocum had heard shouting at him from the shadows the previous night as well as when the Bullseye's front window had been laid to waste. "The trial can take place anytime and won't last long. I guarantee you that."

"I need to know the job is done."

"It is."

"Both men are dead?" the gruff voice asked.

Slocum had gotten to within a few paces of the top of the stairs. As near as he could tell, the other men were still in or near the kitchen but there was no way for him to be certain.

The man with the familiar voice needed a moment to collect himself before replying, "They're dead. That's what you wanted, isn't it?"

"Not what I wanted, Arthur," the gruff voice replied. "But it was necessary. If we're to keep the profits from that job at Misty Creek, there can't be anyone left to point the law in our direction."

"You mean your direction," the other man said as he moved from the back of the house toward the front in a quick series of steps that were so light Slocum hadn't known they were coming.

Rather than risk making the noise it took to step away from the top of the stairs, Slocum bent at the knees and leaned back so his body's weight was centered a bit past the backs of his ankles. It was uncomfortable as hell, but kept most of him out of sight from the floor below.

"I was just hired to clean up the mess you made," the familiar voice continued. "All of the planning and the mess itself falls squarely on your head!"

Heavier steps knocked against the floorboards, but stopped well short of the staircase. "A man in your line of work should know damn well you can't just dip your toe into something like this. You're either all the way in or all the way out, and after killing two decorated Army men, you're in up to your ears!"

"Decorated Army men," the familiar voice scoffed. "That means less and less with every passing year. I'd even wager you were the one to decorate them."

Every muscle in Slocum's legs cried out for mercy, but he maintained his low position. The fire in his knees and ankles grew even hotter when he slowly raised himself up an inch or so while easing himself forward. He had to get a look at the man near the bottom of the stairs, and when he took a risk by coming up a little more, Slocum got what he was after. Sure enough, the man with the familiar voice was the same balding, hawk-nosed fellow in those photographs.

"I did all I could to try and get those two to sign up for the Misty Creek job," the gruffer voice said. "Even when one of Cullen's associates volunteered to lead us to him and Daniel, I didn't want things to turn so bloody. They had their chance to make things right, but chose to remain traitors to their former regiment. Their doing, not mine."

"Well, those two scouts are dead, so I suppose that does mean I'm in this," Vesper said. "It also means I get a bonus."

"Why would you get a bonus?"

"Because I've got John Slocum after me."

"Who the hell is that?"

Vesper shook his head and turned toward the staircase as if he could feel another person's presence there. Stopping short of looking straight up to the limited silhouette Slocum provided, Vesper took hold of the banister and said, "He's not the sort of man that should be trifled with."

"I never even heard his name before," the gruff man said. "I sure as hell didn't trifle with him."

"No, but one of those idiots you hired sure did."

The gruff man surged forward until Slocum could see the wide, battle-scarred face that had been posing with Vesper in one of those pictures. The big man wasn't in uniform now, but he'd worn a major's insignia in the photograph. "Which idiot?" he asked.

"Milt Connoway," Vesper told him. "He and some others hired on as muscle for a gambler in Dodge City. From what I was told, they supplemented their income by luring men into a dark alley, jumping them, and making off with whatever they were carrying. Seems like whatever you were paying them wasn't enough to hold him over."

"God damn it," the major snarled. "Any chance you could kill that asshole?"

"He's locked up in jail. Tricky, but not impossible."

Judging from the sounds he was making, the major was seriously considering the option before he said, "Milt may have shit for brains, but he's no traitor. Has he said anything involving me or what happened at Misty Creek?"

"Not apart from what was already in the newspapers."

Once more, the major stormed forward. And once more, Vesper hardly flinched. "You killed more Injuns than I ever did throughout dozens of campaigns in almost as many territories," the major said.

"You gave the orders."

"And you're retired from active duty. That means if there's anyone who can take the fall if things go south, it's you."

"Things have already gone south," Vesper said. "But not so far that they can't be salvaged. I've had a word with the men that are in jail. As far as they know, they'll be out once the trial is over. They have faith that you would see to that personally."

"Which is why I'm here," the major said. "I just couldn't have those two former scouts of mine here to testify against me."

"Which is why I'm here."

That seemed to calm the major's nerves a bit. "That trial starts tomorrow. I delayed the judge as much as I could through the channels available to me, but there's no stopping it now. Am I to believe the wheels of justice have been sufficiently oiled?"

"You could say that. Apart from the other work I've done, I delivered that payment to Judge Whetuski. Why the hell couldn't you do that yourself?"

"Just covering my tracks," the major proudly replied.

"All right. Since you're so on top of the situation, I take it you brought my money?"

More footsteps made Slocum wince. The major's boots knocked so loudly against the floor that Slocum couldn't be absolutely certain which direction he was going. After what seemed like an eternity, the footsteps faded toward the back and returned to the front room. "Here it is," he said.

It wasn't long before Vesper asked, "All of it?"

"You can count it if you like."

"Nah, I trust you. From what I heard about that Misty Creek job, you and your boys hauled in more than enough to finance a whole lot of track covering. In fact, you shouldn't even miss a bit more."

"What's that supposed to mean, Arthur?"

"It means I've done a good job for you. A hell of a lot better job than those idiots who are cooling their heels behind bars right now. Getting the same cut as them is an insult."

"It's what we agreed on."

"We never agreed on me gunning down two good men."

"How do you know they were so good?"

Slocum had focused so intently on Vesper that he'd all but forgotten the pain burning through his lower half. Since Vesper and the major were eyeing each other as if the rest of the world had dried up and blown away, Slocum was fairly certain his cover was secure.

"Because," Vesper said, "they took a stand against you. They found out about the shipments of gold and silver you'd decided to rob when they crossed Misty Creek. They didn't take the blood money you offered for them to keep quiet, and they didn't take part in the murders you and your men committed to make sure there were no witnesses left to testify that no Pawnee so much as knew about the cargo being shipped through there or had any reason to kill a single soldier. That is," Vesper added, "apart from the reasons you've been giving them throughout your years killing them wholesale."

"You've got some damn nerve to talk to me like that," the major said. "You think you're so high and mighty? You dare to call me out when you've done far worse?"

"You asked how I knew those scouts were good men. I was just giving you an answer."

"And you killed those good men for that money in your hand. What's that make you?"

Without taking so much as a second to think it over, Vesper replied, "It makes me a murdering son of a bitch. I blast men's heads apart before they know they're in my sights. I kill them without needing to know whether their souls are pure or black. I'll tell you what that makes me, sir. It makes me the last man on earth you want to trifle with. Want me to tell you what sort of man you are, sir? You're good at picking your spots for a fight. That's a part of leading men into battle. You recognized a good opportunity when your unit was approached to watch out for those wagons rolling through Pawnee territory carrying such valuable cargo. Taking that cargo made you rich. Pointing the blame at the Indians was easy. Wiping out those settlements along Misty Creek made you look like a man of action while also covering your tracks. I make it my business to know who I'm dealing with. Not to pass judgment, mind you. Just to cover myself in the event a client gets a bit too big for his britches."

"I came with my payment," the major said. "You've got your money."

"That was when the agreed-upon price was for the deaths of two gunmen. To be honest, if you wanted me to kill any of those useless dregs that are sitting in jail now, I would've accepted less. But you wanted me to bring down good men. That's extra."

The major let out a single, scoffing breath. "Why? A fee to ease your conscience?"

"It's just extra. Not a lot more and I know you've got enough to cover it."

In the silence that followed, Slocum wondered if the men downstairs were getting ready to fire at each other. Tension filled the air like fog before the major's voice cut through it. "How much more?"

"An extra fifty percent of the original fee."

"Thirty."

"Forty-five."

"Fine. I'll have it for you after the trial."

"Do you expect me to believe you're not carrying a good chunk of money with you?" Vesper asked.

"Since I'm paying extra, I want you to keep an eye on me just to make certain I leave this town without a scratch."

"You'll be safe here. Anyone in Kansas knows I take care of this place."

"You're a vigilante," the major spat. "Plenty of towns have 'em. Just like rats."

"You're the one who hired me, so you must have known what you were getting."

Slocum didn't need to see the major's face to know there was smug satisfaction on it when he said, "I hired you because this is the place where my boys were brought by those goddamned scouts. You did the job and now you want more money. But," he added before he was reminded yet again of what the extra fee was for, "I suppose that sort of good service deserves reimbursement. I'll pay the extra forty-five percent you want so damn badly. That's for killing those two scouts and for seeing that I get out of town unharmed."

"Who are you so worried about? Slocum?"

"Don't you mind who I'm worried about. That's the task and that's the pay. Take it or leave it."

"I'll take it. As you mentioned," Vesper said, "this is my town. I watch over it no matter what. For the money you're offering, you could strut around wearing a gold crown and still expect to leave without a scratch."

The heavy footsteps thumped once more against the floorboards. "Good. See to it that I do. I'll have the rest of your money in Dodge City. There may be some men there that need to be taken care of as well."

"Who?"

"The gambler that Milt did some side work for. After all the trouble I went through to cover my tracks at Misty Creek, I won't see it undone because of some loose-lipped card-sharp." The major pulled open the door as if he intended on ripping it off its hinges and stormed out.

"Major!"

The steps that had knocked against the house's front porch stopped. When Vesper approached him to talk, Slocum was no longer able to hear what was being said. Rather than get greedy by trying to learn even more, he eased his way into the bedroom, which had the largest window looking out to open ground. He winced every time his boot scraped against the floor, hoping that the sound wouldn't be loud enough to catch either of the other men's attention. When he got to the window, Slocum tried the latch. Just as he'd guessed, it was oiled well enough to come undone with little effort and even less noise. He tried to ease the window open, but could tell it wasn't about to slide very far before scraping against the frame.

Outside, the men were still talking in hushed tones. Slocum guessed he would have at least one more chance to get away from the house without alerting its owner. That chance came when the men finished talking and the major stomped away. His steps knocked against the front porch with authority, sending dull shockwaves through a good portion of the structure. As soon as he heard the first step, Slocum shoved the window open and began climbing out. He made it onto the narrow molding and perched there just long enough to slide the window down again. The major was off the porch by now and Slocum could only guess that Vesper would head inside. The countdown in his head was only slightly off, which meant he hit the dirt beneath the bedroom window a half-second after the front door was closed again.

There wasn't enough time to worry if he'd been heard or

not, so Slocum ignored the stinging sensation in his knees and ran toward Third Avenue. Once there, he stuffed his hands into his pockets, slowed his pace to a leisurely stroll, and walked as if he were simply out to pull some fresh air into his lungs.

As much as he wanted to look back at Vesper's house, Slocum kept strolling toward Main Street. Considering the deadly talents of the man he'd left behind, he expected to hear the crack of a rifle and feel hot lead tear through his back at any moment. Then again, after the shots that Vesper had already pulled off, Slocum doubted he'd have much warning at all before a single round sprayed his brains onto the street.

Seeing the bulky figure strutting ahead of him didn't take his mind completely from the looming specter of death, but it gave Slocum something else to think about. The wide-shouldered frame and overbearing posture looked like the source of the voice he'd heard at Vesper's house, and the powerful gait that rattled the boardwalk along Main Street sure as hell matched the one that had made enough noise to cover his escape. To add insult to injury, the major strutted directly to the Whispering Hills Hotel, where he would surely get one of the best rooms in town.

17

After he'd gotten away from the Vesper house unscathed, Slocum knew he should just lie low and wait for the proper moment to make another move. After hearing about the motive behind the Misty Creek Massacre, the only thing Slocum wanted to do was knock on the doors of each person remotely connected to it and make them pay for what they'd done. He knew more than anyone that spilling all the blood in the world wouldn't bring a single soul back from the grave, but it would at least balance things out for the rest of the world. Nobody should get away with something like that. Nobody.

His first stop was the jailhouse. Slocum was stopped by Teaghan's deputy before he could get close enough to knock on the solid wooden door.

"Just where the hell you think you're goin'?" the young lawman asked.

"I want to have a word with some of those prisoners."

"On whose authority?"

"The sheriff's," Slocum replied. "Just walk me in there so I can ask a few questions."

"Not until I hear from the sheriff."

Almost as frustrated at himself for the fumbling attempt at a bluff as he was by the deputy's reluctance to swallow it, Slocum turned his back to the jailhouse and said, "I'll just have a word with him myself."

Teaghan walked around from the front of his office to intercept him. "You got something to say, Mr. Slocum? I'm right here."

"I've got some questions to ask those prisoners."

"That's what a trial is for."

"This trial may be a farce if those men aren't even being made to answer for the right crimes."

Crossing his arms, Teaghan asked, "What crimes might that be?"

After having too many run-ins with too many crooked lawmen, Slocum was reluctant to expose everything he knew to this one. Although he didn't know with absolute certainty that Teaghan was dirty, he didn't trust the man enough to tip his hand. What he wanted was to get a look at the prisoners' faces when he confronted them with some of the things he'd just heard from the major and Arthur Vesper. One flinch at the wrong time could speak volumes, but only if he was there to see it. "Don't the prisoners get visiting hours?" Slocum asked.

"Not this close to trial."

"What's the harm?"

"Judge Whetuski said there was to be nobody speaking with the prisoners or otherwise doing anything that might taint the case. He don't get out this way very often, and he won't have this trip wasted."

"I'm not about to stand in the way of a trial!" Slocum protested.

If the sheriff's head had been filled with gears, they would have snarled up and started to smoke as he tried to think beyond the simple orders he must have been given.

Finally, Teaghan said, "The judge told me no one's to see the prisoners and that's that."

When Slocum felt someone slap him on the shoulder from behind, he almost wheeled around to punch whoever had decided to get rid of him. Instead of any of the sheriff's or judge's men, he found a determined blond woman who barely even flinched at the motion of Slocum's fist.

"Bethany?" Slocum said as he lowered his arm. "What are you doing here?"

"I was just going to ask you the same thing."

"Maybe you oughta take him home," Sheriff Teaghan said.

The angry fire in Slocum's belly was stoked to new heights, but Bethany wasn't about to let go of his shoulder.

"Come on," she said while pulling him away. "Maybe that's not such a bad idea."

Slocum turned and planted his foot so he wouldn't be dragged one more inch. "I can fight my own battles!"

"So this is a battle now?"

"No."

"Then maybe you should explain it to me."

Emboldened by the proximity of the sheriff and the growing distance between himself and Slocum, the deputy chuckled, "Yeah. Go on and explain it to her."

"Don't let them bait you," she whispered. "It's just a stupid game."

Slocum knew that much already. Of course, his blood was churning so hard through his veins that he might have taken a swing at the next man who made a move at the wrong time.

"Trial's tomorrow, right?" he asked.

"Bright and early," Teaghan replied.

"I'll be there."

"You and most of the town. Best come well ahead of time to get a good seat."

The sheriff didn't have a very big audience, but he was playing up to it as much as possible. Now that he'd had a chance to catch his breath and get his wits about him, Slocum saw the two lawmen for the strutting idiots they were. Also, he reminded himself that all the trouble he'd gone through to keep from drawing too much attention would be undone if he let his temper get the best of him now. When Bethany tugged at him again, he allowed himself to be pulled away from the sheriff's office. Teaghan and his deputy giggled among themselves and swapped what were surely uncomplimentary jibes at Slocum's expense.

"Let them think what they want," Bethany said as she walked beside him and entwined her arm around his. "It'll just be that much more of a surprise when you knock them onto their asses."

"I should trust your judgment."

"It's better than that asshole Whetuski's judgment," she grumbled.

"What's that supposed to mean?"

"Oh, he's all right for the smaller things, but dangle enough cash in front of him and he'll jump higher than a hungry trout. Sometimes it don't even take cash. He gets sick of bedding that clerk of his every now and then, I suppose."

Slocum turned to look at her. "You never mentioned this before."

"Why would I? It's town business and not exactly the sort of thing we're anxious to share with outsiders."

"So I'm no longer an outsider?"

She shrugged and continued down Main. "You deserve the truth."

Slocum followed her to Third Avenue, where they turned north and walked toward her house. "How'd you know I would be at the sheriff's office making a scene?"

"I didn't. I was on my way to the Bullseye and couldn't

help but notice the commotion you were making. Thought I'd step in before you did something you would regret."

"What I wanted to do may not have been the proper thing," Slocum said, "but I doubt I would have regretted it."

"I don't think many people in town would have minded seeing any of those men get put in their place. The law does its job around here, but just barely. More often than not, they're an afterthought once the damage has already been done. The trial is tomorrow," she sighed. "I suppose you'll want to be there to watch?"

"I'll be doing more than watch."

"Then I suggest you keep your nose clean until you can have a seat at the proceedings. Judge Whetuski never has any qualms with pitching folks out of the feed store for the slightest thing."

"Feed store?"

Having arrived at her house, Bethany turned and motioned toward the rest of the town. "Do you see a fancy courthouse anywhere? The feed store is the biggest place other than a barn where the judge can hear his cases. He doesn't like it, which I'm sure will be made clear within the first few seconds of the trial. Come on inside before you get into any more trouble."

Slocum followed her in, but his mind was already working through the next several possible moves he could make to prepare for the next day. As if sensing every one of those plans, Bethany shut the door behind them and moved in to place her hands on either side of his head.

"Stop thinking about it!" she scolded. "I can hear all that nonsense rattling around inside of you like rocks in a tin can."

"I think I should be offended by that."

"Really? And what would you do about it?"

His hands moved reflexively to her hips and she responded by drifting close enough for her breasts to press against him.

Even though he enjoyed the way she slowly ground her hips, he reluctantly told her, "I really should do a few more things."

"Like what?"

"I don't know. Straighten my thoughts to make sure I say the right things tomorrow. Odds are I'll barely get one chance to say my piece."

"You've got all night to think about that. Even though you should get plenty of sleep, I'm sure you'll be up to all hours mulling it over. What else?"

"There may be some men out to kill me."

"Nothing new there. I'll be sure to keep you away from big windows."

"I'm serious," he said in a voice that relayed anything but that sentiment. Her hands had wandered between his legs to stroke his crotch until his body responded to her. She didn't need to wait too long for that.

"So am I," she purred. "Is there seriously something you need to do that you haven't already done?"

"Maybe."

"Is that why you stormed over to the sheriff before you were prepared?" When she didn't get anything but a disgruntled look from Slocum, she smirked and said, "I may not have known you for long, but I know you better than that. I saw the way you were snapping at Teaghan and that poor hapless deputy of his. You weren't any better than a dog pacing at the end of a rope. If I turn you loose now, you'll just get yourself into trouble."

"You think you can keep me in one place?"

She smiled at the challenge and immediately began unbuckling his pants. Her hands reached down to stroke his penis until it was fully rigid. "I've got one or two ideas that might take your mind off of things."

Slocum meant to say something to that, but couldn't get the first word out before she'd knelt in front of him and wrapped her lips around his cock. Bethany kept one hand in place at the base of his shaft, stroking slightly as her tongue swirled around his tip. She opened her mouth in a wide smile as her tongue flicked out to tease him while she looked up into his eyes.

"Trial?" Slocum said as he slid his fingers through her hair. "What trial?"

"That's more like it." Then Bethany moved her hand away so she could devour every inch of his rigid member. She took him into her mouth and sucked him hard until Slocum's knees began to buckle. She seemed more than a little surprised when he pushed her away so he could lift her to her feet. She was even more surprised when he picked her up and carried her to the most convenient room he could find. The front room was small and there were too many stairs between him and the bedroom so he settled for the kitchen. There was a heavy wooden bench there that she used as a table and counter for chopping vegetables. It was sturdy enough to support her weight when she was set on its edge.

"John Slocum, what are you doing?"

He answered that question by hiking up her skirt, peeling off her undergarments, and easing his hands along her thighs. She spread her legs for him and shuddered expectantly when she tossed away his hat so he could place his mouth between her legs. The thatch of hair between her thighs was soft and damp. He found her pussy lips easily and slid his tongue up and down them. By the time he tasted the sensitive nub of her clit, Bethany was gripping the top of his head and bucking against his face.

"God *damn*," she moaned. "I want you inside me now!"

Slocum had barely stood up before she grabbed his shirt and pulled him closer. When Bethany kissed him, his lips were still wet with her moisture. She alternated between slipping her tongue into his mouth and nibbling on his lips. All the while, her entire body squirmed in anticipation while Slocum's hands wandered up and down her legs and sides.

He'd intended on making her wait another couple of seconds just to drive her crazy, but that plan fell through the moment Slocum's cock brushed against the moist spot between her legs. She reached down so that when he eased his hips forward, he slid right where he needed to be. Both of them moaned as he plunged all the way inside her. Bethany wrapped her legs around him while also digging her fingernails into his shoulders. As Slocum started pumping, he reached beneath the folds of her dress to find her tensed buttocks and grab them tightly to keep her in place.

"Yes," she cried as he gripped her harder. "Fuck me!"

Bethany knew what she wanted. Everything from the coarse tone in her voice to the way she wantonly ground her hips in time to his thrusts told him as much. She had no qualms with positioning herself to get the most pleasure from every one of his strokes. A series of little quivers ran through her muscles, and she leaned back to breathlessly watch as Slocum continued to thrust in and out of her. Unwrapping her legs from around him, she propped her heels against the edge of the bench and opened her knees even wider. That way, she could enjoy the sight of him sliding back and forth between her thighs as she reached down to spread herself open even more for him.

Slocum kept one hand clasped to her backside and used the other to massage her breast. When his fingers found her nipple through the thin material of her blouse, Bethany began rubbing herself. "Feels so damn good," she sighed. Her fingers strayed a little lower so she could feel his rigid pole pump into her like a piston.

Before he could get too comfortable in that rhythm, Slocum stepped back and lowered himself onto the floor. "Get your ass over here," he demanded.

Bethany's eyes widened at the sternness of the command and she readily hopped down to approach him. "Yes, sir," she said while pulling off her skirt and tugging at the little buttons of her blouse. By the time she got to him, she was naked from the waist down and her blouse hung open to expose her pert breasts and erect nipples. She straddled Slocum's waist, settling over his stiff manhood.

"What are you waiting for?" he asked.

Rather than allow him to enter her right away, Bethany teased him by brushing the lips of her pussy against his cock. Every time he felt her moist skin slide against him, a shiver worked its way straight down to Slocum's toes.

"You don't get to issue all the orders," she told him. When Slocum reached for her hips to bring her closer, she took his hands in hers and moved them up to her breasts while she settled on top of him. "There now," she said as he began massaging her. "Isn't it nice to take things slower sometimes?"

"Didn't think you were the sort of woman who liked things slow."

"I like them plenty of different ways."

"And I like the sound of that," Slocum said with something of a growl that emanated from the back of his throat.

He was so hard now that he just needed to shift his hips and ease them up in order to slip inside her. The feel of his cock between her lips came as something of a surprise to her, but according to the expression on her face, it was a welcome one. She locked eyes with him and propped herself up on her hands and knees for a few more seconds before finally reaching down to hold him steady as she lowered herself all the way down.

"Have it your way, then," she sighed.

Slocum grabbed her ass in both hands and pumped his cock into her with enough force to make her body stiffen and her next breath emerge in a loud grunt. "You know I will," he said.

Bethany had no more words for a while. All she did was place her hands flat upon his chest and remain in place as Slocum pumped into her. When he eased up, she took over by accepting every inch of him inside her body and grinding her hips in a series of slow circles. It wasn't long before those circles became faster and tighter as she found the spot where he was giving her the most pleasure. Slocum didn't mind staying there one bit.

"That's the way," she said as she straightened her posture and bounced on top of him.

Slocum could barely hear her over the rush of blood coursing throughout his entire body. His fingertips dug into the soft flesh of her hips as he pounded inside her again and again. Her pussy was slick and wrapped around him perfectly. When she ground against him, Slocum was able to pump even deeper between her legs. Her body started to tremble with another approaching climax, but he beat her to the punch. With one more thrust, he exploded inside her and his grip loosened.

"Just a little more," she pleaded. "A little more."

Even though Slocum was barely moving, Bethany bounced on him as if she were taming a bucking bronco. She leaned her head back and tossed her hair while riding his cock with mounting urgency. Slocum didn't know if he could stand much more, but she finally let out a powerful cry and was overcome by an intense orgasm. When it passed, she wilted and rested on top of him.

"Glad I found you," she sighed.

"Yeah. Me, too."

Slocum caught his breath and started getting up, but Bethany wasn't cooperating. "Come on," he said while lifting her up a bit. "You've got to at least let me get to my feet."

She reluctantly complied, but didn't take more than a half step away from him. When she saw him move toward the pants he'd kicked off somewhere along the way, she asked, "Where do you think you're going?"

"Same place I was going before. Things to do and not a lot of time to get them done."

"Did you come up with something more important than the last time you tried to explain yourself?"

He picked her up and set her down to one side so she was no longer blocking his way. "I appreciate what you're saying, but I don't have to explain myself. Not to you and not to anyone."

"That means you haven't come up with anything better," she said while hopping in front of him. When he reached out to move her aside again, Bethany grabbed his arm with a surprising amount of strength. "What I told you before still stands. I'm not about to let you go back out and kick up any more dust."

"The sheriff didn't catch all of the men who shot at me through the Bullseye window. That means a killer could still be after me and if he finds me here . . ."

Rather than allow him to talk his way out of that house, Bethany said, "If he knew you were here, he would have taken a shot at you already."

"You don't know that!"

"And you don't know otherwise. Come along with me," she said while leading him toward the stairs.

Slocum still wanted to get back outside, where he could try and gather more information, hunt down some gunmen or . . . he hated to admit . . . cause some more trouble. Bethany was right. He was as ready as he was going to be for the next day's trial, and whatever he might stir up before then could potentially make things worse. Also, even if he'd decided to start all the trouble Culbertson could handle, he doubted he could escape Bethany's grip.

She led him up the stairs toward her bedroom. "You're not going anywhere for a while," she promised. "After you catch your breath, I've got plenty more for you to do."

Watching her naked backside twitch as she climbed the stairs in front of him made it difficult for Slocum to come up with one good reason why he should be anywhere else.

18

Despite Bethany's best efforts to drain every bit of steam he had, Slocum woke up bright and early the next morning and was out the door before the sun had fully crested the horizon. Since he was alone in bed when his eyes had first opened, he knew he wasn't going to beat her to the Bullseye. Sure enough, when he got to the saloon, she was at her place in the kitchen and every table was filled.

"John!"

Slocum partially recognized the voice, but something about it didn't seem right. He glanced toward the back of the room to find Slick behind the bar waving at him. The balding barkeep had been the one to shout, but it was the first time he hadn't sounded perturbed about something.

"Go on back to the kitchen," Slick said when Slocum returned his wave. "She's waiting for ya."

There were so many customers in the place that he had a rough time navigating through them to get to the swinging kitchen doors. As soon as he stepped through them, Bethany said, "Don't worry about finding a seat. You can eat back here. You didn't already have breakfast yet, did you?"

She stood at a stove with her sleeves rolled up and sweat pouring down her face. The only time he'd seen her more flushed was the night before.

"No, I didn't eat," he replied. "I'm not really hungry, though."

"Of course you are. I know you worked up an appetite." There were a few other workers back there with her, but she didn't seem to care what they thought when they smirked and looked at her and Slocum.

"I don't have time to eat before the trial anyway," he said. "Where's it being held?"

"At the feed store on North Virginia. It's a short walk from here, but you ain't leaving without getting something to eat. I'm making some ham steaks and biscuits. It won't kill you to get something in your belly along with some coffee."

"Where's the coffee?"

"At the bar."

"Great," Slocum said as he reached for the plate she was hastily preparing. There was already a biscuit on there, which he picked up and ripped in half. Once she placed a thick cut of ham onto the plate, he picked that up as well.

"Use a damn fork, you savage!" she said.

"Don't need one," Slocum replied while placing the ham between the biscuit halves and taking a bite. "Not enough time. This is just fine the way it is." He showed her a smile covered in crumbs and left the kitchen.

"Damn savage," she grumbled.

Slocum took another couple bites from his sandwich as he crossed the main room. He got plenty of puzzled glances as he made his way to the bar and knocked to catch Slick's attention.

"What's that you got there?" the barkeep asked before Slocum's knuckles were completely off the wooden surface.

"Something that'll go great with coffee," Slocum replied. Not anxious to engage in more conversation with so many other customers to tend to, Slick poured some coffee into a tin cup. Slocum picked it up and headed for the door.

"Bring my cup back!" Slick shouted.

One of the customers bellowed, "Whatever that ham thing was, I'll take one, too!"

Before he could wonder if he'd started a new trend, Slocum had downed most of his sandwich. As he walked along Main Street, he alternated between eating and sipping his coffee. Once the last bit of ham steak was gone, he could see the crowd gathering outside Wheeler's Feed and Seed. There couldn't have been more than a dozen or so people outside, but compared to the rest of the quiet town, it might as well have been a night at the coliseum. Slocum took one last sip of coffee before setting the cup down against a water trough and quickening his pace.

"Everybody stand back!" Sheriff Teaghan bellowed from the front door of the feed store. "Just stand back unless you're part of the proceedings. How many of you are part of the proceedings?"

The crowd's chatter died down to a low murmur as two hands were slowly raised.

"Is that just because you know one of the men in jail or because you were actually part of the case that's being heard?"

Both hands were lowered.

"Thought so," the sheriff huffed. "All of you stand back, and when the time comes, you'll enter in an orderly manner. When we run out of seats, you'll wait outside. I take it some of you have cases of your own to be heard by Judge Whetuski?"

Several hands went up.

"Good. When this first one is done, the rest of you will be ushered inside in an orderly manner."

Slocum had his doubts that anything close to orderly could be salvaged from this mess, but he let the town conduct its affairs in its own way. When the sheriff started to turn his back on everyone and go inside, Slocum shouted, "What about me?"

"Didn't I just ask for a show of hands?"

"Didn't you just look straight at me already?"

The lawman rolled his eyes and motioned for Slocum to come forward.

The inside of the store was mostly cleared out. Several long tables had been moved to one side of the large room and another table had been topped with a clean black cloth complete with bunting more suited for the Fourth of July. Three chairs were set up behind that table, and a smaller square table was set up beside that. Slocum's guess was that the smaller table was the witness stand. The rest of the room was filled by three rows of mismatched chairs hemmed in by a stack of sacked oats and a counter filled with bridles topped by a rusty cash register. Either the owner of the store insisted on premium seats or someone snuck in, because an elderly couple already sat front and center at the head of the gallery.

"Have a seat there," the sheriff said while pointing to the lone chair behind the square table. "Judge Whetuski is on his way."

Slocum did as he was told, and the deputy approached him before his backside could get settled upon the uneven surface.

"Hand over your guns," the young lawman said.

Having learned his lesson in Dodge City, Slocum was only carrying the .44 and had left the .38 in his saddlebag in the event he might need it. By the time he handed over the pistol, folks were being let in to fill the gallery seats. The proceedings got under way as soon as the chairs were filled.

"All rise for the Honorable Judge Aaron Whetuski," the pretty clerk announced as she entered through a door marked, STORAGE AND PRIVITE OFICES.

Whetuski walked in from the storage room wearing a

flowing black robe and carrying a thick volume of law texts as if it were his Bible. A gavel was already placed in front of the middle chair at the long table. He sat behind the little hammer, rapped it a few times upon the table, and called for order. A side door that must have led to an alley was opened to allow a strange procession to join the proceedings. At the front of the line was Sheriff Teaghan, who held a chain that was looped through shackles secured around the wrists of Milt Connoway and six other men. Slocum didn't recognize four of the men. Wes and Benjamin were among the prisoners as well, wearing their bandages as if they'd gotten their wounds on a battlefield. The deputy was near the end of the row of prisoners, and the caboose of the shuffling train was a man dressed in full military regalia whom Slocum recognized as the man who'd met Arthur Vesper at his home. Everything from the Army medals and insignias, all the way down to the ornate buttons on his coat, was polished to a golden sheen. Slocum couldn't help being impressed by the sight. The locals in the gallery were positively awestruck.

Milt and two other prisoners were separated from the other shackled men and held at gunpoint against a wall away from the participants of the trial and the public gallery. Both lawmen stood watch over them while the Army officer took a seat at the far end of the long table.

"Court is now in session," the clerk said. "First matter on the docket is the State of Kansas versus Milton Connoway, Jonathan Hendricks, and Samuel Nading."

"What is the charge?" Whetuski asked.

"Multiple counts of first-degree murder in connection with the deaths of Pawnee Indians at three villages along Misty Creek. We are hearing this case at the behest of a representative of the United States Army. Since the military has declined to press further charges in the matter, it has been handed over to this court."

"I've read the report. I believe we have an expert witness present to add some further details."

"We do, Your Honor." Motioning toward the officer, the clerk announced, "Major Dwight Garrison, currently in command of several outposts in Kansas and Nebraska."

"You were present for the Misty Creek slayings, Major Garrison?" Whetuski asked.

The major stood at attention with enough authority to make everyone in the gallery straighten their posture. "I was, Your Honor."

"Can you explain anything that happened that wasn't covered in your report?"

"There was a string of attacks in the vicinity of Misty Creek. My regiment was given the task to investigate and provide protection for travelers in that area. Several more coaches were attacked and everyone traveling on them was brutally killed in a manner my men and I have become familiar as being Pawnee tactics."

The gallery shuddered.

"When the Pawnee continued to attack civilians as well as robbing valuable shipments for what we can only assume was the furthering of their own goals," Garrison continued, "I led a group of men to exact justice in a way that was the only method those savages could understand."

"Which was?"

"We tracked the killers to where they lived and tried to take them peacefully. When they resisted, my men and I defended ourselves. The fight escalated until we had no choice but to set a torch to their camp to smoke them out. Regretfully, some Pawnee that weren't involved in the killings may have been lost."

"May have been lost?" Slocum asked. "Women and children were killed. It was the Misty Creek Massacre! It was in the newspapers, for God's sake."

"Stories get trumped up by the press all the time," Garrison said with a wave of his hand. "A soldier's work has nothing to do with any of that."

"This court is only interested in facts," Whetuski proclaimed. "You may continue, Major."

"There's nothing more to say," Garrison said. "We completed our duty, unfortunate as it may have been, and the incident was blown up by the overzealous pen of some reporter."

"Why are these three men standing in front of me?" Whetuski asked while motioning to the three prisoners that had been singled out.

Major Garrison looked over at the men in chains as if they were standing at an award ceremony. "These men were granted a leave from their duties to recover from the events at Misty Creek. Some more men under my command, men who were too cowardly to carry out the orders they'd been given, took it upon themselves to hunt them down and accuse them of murder. Those charges are preposterous, and I am here to say so personally."

Slocum stood up and roared, "That's a damn lie!"

Without casting an eye in Slocum's direction, Judge Whetuski said, "Since this man refuses to wait for his turn, kindly swear him in."

The clerk approached Slocum with a Bible in hand. When Slocum placed his hand upon it, she recited, "Do you swear to tell the truth, the whole truth, and nothing but the truth, so help you God?"

"Yes."

Now Whetuski deigned to look at him. "Your name, sir?"

"John Slocum."

"What is your account of what happened at Misty Creek, Mr. Slocum?"

"I wasn't there, but I was with—"

"You weren't there?" Whetuski asked.

"No, sir. I brought Milt Connoway into custody along with Daniel Garner."

"Daniel Garner is one of the cowardly deserters I mentioned, Your Honor," Garrison explained.

Before the two highest-ranked officials in the room could banter any more, Slocum said, "Daniel and another man named Cullen witnessed the Misty Creek killings and knew they had nothing to do with any Indian attacks. He said those villages were put to the torch to cover robberies committed by Army officers. In that time, I've discovered Major Garrison to be one of the officers who was killing innocent people to try and cover his own crimes."

Once again, the gallery erupted into a cascade of excited whispers. This was just the thing they'd hoped to see. The judge slammed his gavel on the table and shouted, "Order in my court! Mr. Slocum, these are serious charges."

"Indeed they are, sir."

"What evidence do you have to back them up?"

"I'm here as a witness. Major Garrison hired a local man named Arthur Vesper to kill both Cullen and Daniel."

"You saw this?"

"Not the hiring, but—"

"Then you have no reason to testify. What about the deaths of Cullen and Daniel?"

"I did see that, Your Honor."

"Then that is a matter that shall be decided separately once charges have been properly filed, witnesses called, and a man is in custody."

"Arthur Vesper lives here in town," Slocum said.

"After these proceedings, I'll look into possible cause in having him brought into official custody," Whetuski said. "Do you have anything to say in the matter of the killings at Misty Creek?"

"Anything more than they were murders to cover robberies by Major Garrison and these men here instead of anything close to any kind of military action done under legal orders?"

"Unless you have any concrete evidence to show or were

present at the time when the crimes were committed, anything you have to say on the matter is hearsay," the judge told him. "Since there are no witnesses to dispute the claims with any accuracy and there is no evidence to say that these men were anything but soldiers acting on behalf of—"

"There aren't any witnesses because that son of a bitch had them killed!" Slocum said while leveling a finger at Garrison. "I'll take you to their graves if you don't believe me!"

"The deaths of . . ."

"Daniel Garner and a Mr. Cullen," the clerk said when the judge floundered for his next line.

"Yes," Whetuski said. "Those deaths are another matter and shall be addressed in a separate trial. As for this matter, seeing as how there is no evidence or *proper* witnesses, this case is dismissed."

"Dismissed?"

"Mr. Slocum, remove yourself from the witness stand and hold your tongue before you're charged with contempt," Whetuski commanded.

"This is bullshit! Those assholes killed innocent men! That one there jumped me in Dodge City! Won't he even stand trial for that?"

Whetuski sifted through the short stack of papers that had been tucked in his arm along with his legal book. "I don't see anything here about a robbery in Dodge City. That would have to be tried there, obviously."

Slocum stood up and looked around as if he were in a dream. Much like other dreams he'd had, he felt as if he were falling end over end without actually moving from his spot. The harder he searched for someone to speak up on his side or even on the side of reason, the less he found. Anyone who would have filled that role was now filling one of several holes in the gritty Kansas dirt.

"The next case on the docket, Miss Sallow?" Whetuski calmly said.

The clerk looked down her nose at her own papers and declared, "George Finley versus Nicholas Hague. Mr. Hague is charged with stealing fourteen dollars from under Mr. Finley's mattress."

"That's truly all that's going to be done about all the Pawnee that were killed?" Slocum asked.

"Dead Indians are not the primary concern of this court," Whetuski replied. "Rumors, either from you or a newspaper, aren't either. Dodge City matters shall be addressed in Dodge City."

"What about the deaths of those two soldiers at the hand of Arthur Vesper?" Slocum asked. "That happened right outside of town and I was there to see it."

"I'm Arthur Vesper."

Slocum glared at the man who spoke those words and immediately recognized the fellow who stood up at the back of the gallery as the hawk-nosed marksman whose house he'd visited.

"Do you know about the charges that are being levied against you?" the judge asked.

"Never heard about it before in my life, Your Honor."

"I can speak on behalf of Mr. Vesper," Major Garrison declared. "He is an officer of impeccable character and I'll have words with anyone who decides to treat him otherwise. As for you, Mr. Slocum, leveling such serious charges against a man in my position is *not* something that should be taken lightly."

"Since there is a complaint to be filed, I'll expect Sheriff Teaghan to see to it that Mr. Vesper remains in town until I can return to hear the evidence on that matter. Is there any further evidence in this case?"

"Your Honor," Slocum said in the most civil tone he could produce, "these men cannot be set loose. They're murderers."

"They're soldiers," Garrison said.

"And that man is a liar," Slocum added while pointing at the major.

"No more evidence is forthcoming so these men are free to go." Whetuski smacked his gavel against the table with enough force to rattle every board. "Case dismissed."

19

The remaining cases were heard before lunch. As it turned out, a matter involving a dispute between two neighbors' property lines took longer than the cases of the Misty Creek Massacre or the missing fourteen dollars. Once the judge handed down his verdict without so much as an attempt to form a jury, the gallery was dismissed and the town went about its business.

Slocum received his .44 along with a stern warning, which did nothing to deter him from lurking about Main Street for a glimpse at the men he was after. Major Garrison was easy to find as he strutted back to the Whispering Hills. After a few minutes, Slocum followed in his wake. The preening bastard sat at his table in the hotel's little dining area like an oversized monument placed in an undersized courtyard.

When Slocum stepped into the dining room, Milt jumped to his feet and placed his hand upon an empty holster.

"Easy, Milt," Garrison said without any of the pretense that had dripped from every syllable when he'd been in the feed store. "Surely Mr. Slocum isn't stupid enough to try anything violent."

"I owe this fucker," Milt snarled.

"I may have been misinformed," Slocum replied. "At least, about the Misty Creek thing. But we both know you got things started between us when you jumped me back in Dodge City."

Milt accepted that quietly, but came back with, "You took your money and things back, along with *my* guns."

"Here," Slocum said as he eased the .44 from his holster using a thumb and forefinger upon the grip. "Take it."

"What about the other one?"

The .38 was tucked at the small of Slocum's back, but he told him, "I can get it to you later. Right now, there's more important things to discuss."

Before Milt could unleash whatever obscenities he had in mind, Major Garrison said, "You hired on with a cheating gambler in Dodge, Milt. Way I see it, you would've wound up in jail one way or another. Since you cracked Mr. Slocum when he wasn't looking, you two should be square."

Reluctantly, Milt backed off.

"What brings you here, Mr. Slocum?" Garrison asked. "Can't be the food."

"No. It's about what you said at the trial." Slocum removed his hat and held it clasped in front of him. "I can't afford any official trouble with the Army or certain other governmental bodies."

Garrison smirked in a way that made him look like any other employer, land baron, lawman, or authority figure who wielded his power like a club and was only truly happy when someone flinched in his presence. "Keep your nose clean and stay out of my sight."

"I want a guarantee I won't have any official trouble, sir."

"Can't do that, son."

"What if I gave you something to settle up for good?"

Slocum said. "Something valuable enough for us to part ways as if we never met?"

"What sort of thing are you talking about?"

Stepping forward caused all three of the gunmen to reach for the pistols that had so recently been returned after being set loose from their shackles. Garrison motioned for them to let Slocum get closer, but close in around him like an encroaching wall. Every one of Slocum's muscles tensed as he prepared himself to reach for the hidden .38.

"I'm talking about the evidence that judge was so hot to see this morning," Slocum whispered.

"What evidence?"

"I don't know exactly what it was. Daniel was carrying it and Cullen had some of his own. I only rode with Daniel for a short time, so he didn't tell me everything, but he and Cullen had plenty to talk about when they met outside of town. That is, before Vesper gunned them both down."

Nobody twitched at that, which told Slocum he'd been correct in assuming things between Vesper and the Army men were anything but smooth.

"I can't think of what either of those men might have had," Garrison stated.

Slocum wrung his hands as well as the hat he held. "I don't know what it was either, but they were both anxious to get it here for today's trial. And Vesper was even more anxious to get it away from them. Why would he do that? Wasn't he working for you?"

Garrison twitched. "What do you propose, Mr. Slocum?"

"Let me get those items from Vesper and show them to you. After you see them, you can decide for yourself whether or not they're worth cleaning the slate between you and me. I know where he lives. Just give me a chance to get those things from him and show you."

If Garrison had any clue that Slocum had been at Vesper's house before, he was hiding it expertly now. This was the perfect moment for him to mention such a thing, and he didn't show the first sign of doing so. "You intend on walking in there to fetch those items?"

"I know what I'm looking for. I saw the bundle in Daniel's possession every step of the way during the ride from Dodge." Despite the vagueness of his claim, Slocum could tell it was being swallowed hook, line, and sinker.

"I don't intend on waiting for long."

"Good. I'll tell you where the house is. I'll go in alone, but you're more than welcome to watch to make sure I don't run away."

"I don't give a damn where you go," Garrison said unconvincingly. "But for the sake of speeding things along, we'll do this your way. If I like what you bring me, I'll forget we ever met."

"Sounds great, sir," Slocum said as he reached across the table to shake Garrison's hand. "I'll get that evidence and toss it out a window so you or one of your boys here can collect it."

"And what about Vesper?"

"I'll take care of him," Slocum replied. "I take it that wouldn't be a problem?"

"Not at all."

Keeping himself from punching the major in the face took more restraint than Slocum thought he possessed.

Getting into Vesper's house was a whole lot easier the second time around. Rather than try any fancy sneaking, he walked up to the front door and knocked.

Vesper answered right away by opening the door a crack and grunting, "What the hell do you want?"

"It's not what I want," Slocum said. "It's what Major Garrison wants."

"What's that?"

"He sent me here to get the money back."

"What money?"

Slocum shrugged. "That's what he said." When Vesper tried to shut the door, Slocum kept it open by jamming his boot between it and the frame. "You should really let me inside. There's some things you need to hear."

"Move your damn foot or lose it."

"I know what you did outside of town. Lucky for you I barely knew those men. Looking back, I see you're a man who keeps his head on straight when the bullets start to fly. That's why you picked off those two soldiers first."

"It's why I tried to get you to leave town in the first place."

"Exactly. We're both businessmen. I hate to see someone get double-crossed when they were just trying to conduct business the best way possible."

"What double-cross?"

If there was one thing that tied all murderers, thieves, and outlaws together, it was suspicion of their fellow man. Being men who were untrustworthy themselves, they trusted no one. It was why simple folks and children were ready to believe whatever they heard. People simply measured the rest of the world against their own example, and so far that notion was being proven right in front of Slocum's eyes. Vesper's face reflected all manner of unkind thoughts that flickered through his head like a disturbing picture show.

"Can I come in?" Slocum asked.

Slowly, Vesper stood aside. When he opened the door, he revealed the sawed-off shotgun he'd been holding in his other hand in the event he decided to blast a hole through the door as well as anyone standing beyond it. Once Slocum had come into the foyer, Vesper snapped, "That's far enough. State your business."

"Did Major Garrison hire you to kill those men?"

Although Vesper's sunken face was much more difficult to read than Garrison's, Slocum couldn't see anything to worry about just yet. If Vesper knew Slocum had been spying on his earlier conversation with the major, he could have pointed that out right then. After all, he was the one holding the shotgun and didn't seem to have much fear in his heart. Vesper was a cold man cut from a colder chunk of granite.

"Those men were turncoats and outlaws," Vesper replied.

"My guess is that Garrison did a little research, maybe asked around to some of his friends or to the sheriff himself, so he could find someone with your qualifications. He gave you this job, but didn't know what kind of specialist you were. Probably thought you were some local gunman no better than any number of hired killers to be found in any number of towns."

"Get to your point."

"Garrison underestimated me the same way," Slocum said. "He thinks he can order me around like another one of his brainless lackeys. When he asked me to get his money back, I thought you deserved better than a bullet when you weren't looking."

"Even though that's what I gave to those two you were riding with?"

Now was Slocum's turn to keep from flinching. Although Vesper's face barely changed, he knew he was being studied by the sharpshooter for any hint of a reaction to that statement. If Slocum was looking for a chance to get in close for some quick payback, it could show in the slightest tremor at the corner of one eye upon hearing such casual mention of Daniel's and Cullen's deaths.

"Yes," Slocum replied with a fair amount of ominous intensity. "Even though you also tried to kill me that same night."

Vesper grinned, and his expression was as appealing as the smile found on a corpse that had gotten its lips peeled off by vultures. "And you took some liberal shots at me. We both slipped away from each other that night and I allowed you to keep breathing. Call it professional courtesy on my part. I see I wasn't mistaken in granting you that much."

Now Slocum was completely certain he hadn't been spotted the other night when eavesdropping on the conversation between Vesper and Garrison.

"Still," Vesper added, "there's no way for me to know if you're telling me the truth about the major. He doesn't have much reason to lie to me about our arrangement."

"I couldn't tell you about his reasons, but he's waiting for me to bring out that money and I don't think he expects you to hand it over willingly. If you want proof, take a look through a window that looks out to the open side of your property line."

Vesper used the shotgun to motion for Slocum to head to the side of the house facing away from the rest of town. "Open the window," he said once they reached a bedroom with a total of two pieces of furniture in it. Slocum did as he'd been told and could immediately see the row of horsemen waiting just under a hundred yards away.

"That's—"

"I can see who it is," Vesper snapped as if his eyesight was being called into question. For a marksman of his caliber, that was one hell of an insult. "What are they waiting for?"

"A shot. After that, I'm to toss out the money I collected and ride away. They'll send someone to collect it. Still don't believe me? There's one sure way to find out."

Vesper drew a breath and walked out of the room. Slocum heard some rummaging sounds, and when Vesper returned, he was carrying a small sack of flour. "Take that pillow off the bed and remove the case." When Slocum carried out the order, Vesper tossed the flour to him. "Put that in the case."

Before the flour hit the bottom of the pillowcase, a single pistol shot blasted through the room. Slocum had been expecting it, but still jumped when it happened. Vesper had drawn and fired without making a sound.

"Now toss it out."

Slocum nodded, walked over to the window, and opened it. Behind him, Vesper retreated like a shadow dispelled by a moving lantern.

One of the distant riders approached the house. It was Milt and he brought his horse to a stop so he could climb down from the saddle and pick up the case. "This what you were supposed to get?" he asked.

"Yeah," Slocum said. "Get it away from here quickly. I think someone heard the shot. Also, you'd better not look inside."

"Don't have to tell me that much. The major wants this all to himself." With that, Milt climbed into his saddle and rode away with the pillowcase in his grasp.

"Son of a bitch," Vesper snarled as he reemerged from the shadows of the next room. Instead of the shotgun, he was now holding a long rifle that looked to have been given several modifications. Slocum's guess about the wild turns of a suspicious mind were proven correct as Vesper placed the rifle stock to his shoulder and fired from the bedroom's doorway. His first shot shattered the window and clipped Milt. The second popped Milt's head like a melon before he had a chance to fall halfway off his horse.

With calm precision, Vesper levered in another round, fired, levered, and fired until he'd sent eight shots through the bedroom window. Slocum stood to one side, doing his best to stay out of the line of fire and not draw any attention. Outside, a few shots were fired at the house, but were cut short amid the sounds of dying men hitting the ground and the excited whinnies of panicked horses. The quiet that followed was too complete for there to have been any survivors.

Reaching around to the small of his back, Slocum drew the .38 and pointed it at Vesper. "That's enough, Arthur. It's over."

The only part of Vesper to move was his eyes as they

darted to his left to get a look at Slocum. "You want the money for yourself?"

"I want to see justice done and you exceeded my expectations where that was concerned."

"Justice with a flair for drama, I see. Otherwise, you could have done it yourself."

"Major Garrison wasn't going to let me or anyone else get close enough to do the job," Slocum explained. "He may have even had you covering him for all I know. Then there's the trouble that comes along with executing a decorated officer of the United States Army. Even though the world is a better place without a murdering piece of shit like Garrison, I've got enough trouble following me around without a charge like that tacked on. Now that you mention it, though, having you kill him does seem right somehow."

"What makes you think I won't kill you anyway?" Vesper asked.

"Because you're a long-range shooter and my specialty is up close. At a hundred yards or more, it's all your game. In close quarters, looking another man straight in the eyes, it's mine and you know it."

"So what are you waiting for?"

Slocum shrugged. "Professional courtesy?" He lowered the .38 and almost immediately Vesper snapped his rifle toward him. Slocum's arm sprang up again so he could fire from the hip. His round caught Vesper through the heart, killing him instantly. Deadweight hit the floor, but Slocum took Vesper's rifle just in case the ghoulish vigilante had one last gulp of air in his lungs.

He took a look out the window to see that Garrison and all the men with him had been dropped. Running through similar motions that had allowed him to sneak away from the house the first time, Slocum circled around the Proctor home and behind the abandoned house on the corner. By the time he made it back to Main Street, there was so much commotion pointed in the direction from which the shots had been fired that Slocum was able to slip into the ruckus like just another concerned citizen.

After putting the turmoil behind him, it was less than an hour before he collected his things, saddled his horse, snapped his reins, and sneered, "Case dismissed."

Watch for

SLOCUM AND THE HIGH-RAILS HEIRESS

398th novel in the exciting SLOCUM series
from Jove

Coming in April!

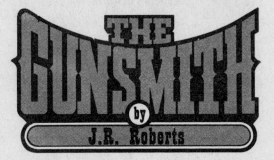
M11G0610